Town of Horror

Written by James Milliken

Chapter 1

Cold wind blew on the ominous morning and three brave but unaware souls entered the cursed town which was plagued with unfortunate problems. However, little do these three know…This town, that's called Ghost, has horrors the likes no one has ever seen or heard of before. Behind every corner…Down every dark alley…In the polluted streets…Sinister atmosphere and people await their next victims for the Key to find the Lock then all hell will break loose and a king…will be revived.

48 hours earlier…

On a beautiful Sunday evening, a loving couple enjoy their day at the park. A young thirty year old man and his beautiful twenty eight year old girlfriend, can be seen taking a memorial photo together at a local park bench…

"Matthew? Aren't you done yet?" Sarah asked as she waited for her boyfriend to set up the camera to take a picture with both of them in the park.

"Just give me a sec babe. Damn thing isn't cooperating with me today." Matthew said as he messed with the tripod for the camera.

"Ugh! Take any longer and we will lose the light! It's already 7:30 and the sun is setting!" Sarah complained.

"Almost there…Got it!" Mathew said as he hurried over to Sarah before the timer took the picture.

"Say cheese." Sarah said with a warm smile as the picture was taken by the camera.

"Let me look and see." Mathew said as went over to the digital camera to look at the picture that was taken and Sarah followed.

"Looks great. Though I think your eyes need to look at the camera and not my boobs." Sarah joked.

"Sh-Shut up. I wasn't looking at your chest!" Mathew said as he blushed from embarrassment.

"You're lie says one thing but your camera tells it all. Hahahaha." Sarah laughed.

"Whatever…We should probably head back. Don't you need to head home tomorrow afternoon?" Mathew asked.

"Yeah. I'm already packed and got my bus ticket. Mom probably can't wait to see me after ten years. I left town when was eighteen but never had the chance to see her or my Dad since." Sarah said in a slightly depressed tone of regret.

"I'm sure they would understand. Your work took you two counties over and you've been busy working at the hospital while going to school to become a nurse practitioner. Plus you've been keeping in touch with them with phone calls. So it's not like you've been neglecting them." Mathew said as he put Sarah's worries to rest as she smiled at his comforting words.

"You're right. I'm sure they don't hate me or anything. It just sucks you can't come along." Sarah said with a sly smile hinting on a romantic get-away.

"You know my work is important too. I just became a police officer two years ago and now I have more work than what I know what to do with." Mathew said and he folded up the tripod and put away the camera in the car the two drove in.

"I know… Well at least it's just for a week and then I will be back." Sarah said as she embraced her loving boyfriend as the two shared a warm hearted kiss.

The couple was about to head home but Mathew had a strange feeling that they were being watched before they left the park. However, Mathew shrugged it off and got into the car. When the couple got home, they went to bed since Sarah had to leave early in the morning and Mathew had work.

The very next day, Mathew waved goodbye to his girlfriend as she left in the bus driving west bound. Sarah waved goodbye too and she was gone with the bus moments later. Mathew then got back into his police car and drove back to the station.

When Mathew arrived back to the station, there was a loud suspect that was detained and put into the holding cell with a bunch of other people whom also got arrested for different crimes.

"GHOST!!! Stay away from GHOST!!" The man shouted.

"Be quiet!" An officer yelled as he banged on cell bar near the man with a nightstick.

"What's his problem?" Mathew asked one of the ladies that was working at a desk for dispatch.

"Oh he's been arrested for possession of LSD and other drugs. He tried to get rid of the evidence by swallowing it but puked it up five minutes later. He could still be feeling side-effects of the drugs." The lady explained but still the man was shouting about staying away from Ghost.

"Hm. Sarah said her parents lived in a town called Ghost…Probably just a coincidence." Mathew thought as he walked over to his sergeant's desk…

"Hey Sergeant." Mathew greeted.

"Matt. Nice timing Lt gave me some orders to pass on to you." The police sergeant said as he handed Mathew the papers for his assignment.

"What…What is this?" Mathew asked.

"Apparently a small secluded town called Ghost is in need of some sort of backup temporally. I know it's out of our jurisdiction but the lieutenant got the greenlight from the state to send three officers over there for about a week or so." The sergeant said.

Mathew didn't want to tell his fellow officers that his girlfriend Sarah was staying in Ghost for a while because they might take him off the case due to conflict of interests. So he kept his mouth shut about the fact. Instead Mathew questioned the need of his department's involvement in this town…

"So why are three of us going to Ghost anyways? Can't their police unit handle their own crimes?" Mathew asked.

"It's not a matter of crime being committed…It's about keeping the piece since there is some sort of strange cult that's obsessed with something called a demon king. I have no damn idea what these lunatics are doing but the local authorities are few and have asked many neighboring departments for help but all said no…until now with us." The sergeant said.

"Hmm…ok then. So who's coming with me?" Mathew asked as he saw the sergeant pull out files of the two other officers.

"Corporal James Smith who's in command and Patrolman Susy Miller your equal ranked officer." The sergeant said.

"When do we head out?" Mathew asked.

"Tomorrow o-six hundred. You three are to be expected to arrive within a few hours and will have no radio contact with us during your time spent during this week. Work with the local department to quell this group and put an end to this. Now you are dismissed for the day. Head home, pack up, and get some rest." The sergeant said and Mathew nodded as he left for the day…

During that night, Mathew couldn't sleep as he laid in bed thinking about going to Ghost and possibly seeing his girlfriend. He then thought he would bring it up as a surprise if they were to meet in the town so it would erase suspicion between his fellow officers.

The next morning Mathew finished getting ready with his gear and packed uniforms and nighttime clothing for the next week. As he holstered his sidearm, he heard a car horn outside beeping. He looked and saw his two partners for the next week in the police car waiting for him to come. Mathew grabbed his gear and bag then headed out of his house…

"Come on slow poke! I want to get this over with so I can get my bonus check." James said in the driver's seat while in the backseat was Susy and she wasn't looking Mathew's way as she fidgeted nervously.

"I'm coming. Looks like I'm getting shotgun, huh?" Mathew said.

"Nope. Sorry pal but I got paperwork up here so you're just gonna have to sit in the back with your future spouse." James joked and laughed.

"I-I DON'T LIKE HIM LIKE THAT OKAY!? S-Stop saying that!" Susy protested as she madly blushed from embarrassment.

"Quit with jokes James. We're supposed to be on the clock remember?" Mathew said as he jumped in the backseat with Susy.

"Yeah yeah. Let's just get this over with." James said as he put the car in gear and headed west bound…

As the three were driving towards their destination, there was an awkward silence in the car. Mathew decided to break the quiet moment.

"So James…Sergeant says you are in command on this little week long trip." Mathew said.

"Yeah. It's not like I wanted to be but I needed the extra money so I signed up. Susy did the same once she heard lieutenant picked you to come as well." James said.

"That's not true! I-I only came to help our fellow police officers in need. Even if we are city police and they're just a small town department." Susy said.

"Well I'm grateful either way." Mathew said with a smile. He knew Susy had a crush on him but never return the feeling because he was already seeing someone else. However, he always kept his personal life private.

"Anyways. Did the lieutenant give us any more details on this place we are going to?" Susy asked.

"From what I've been told, it's an old timely town since the beginning of the country's independence but never kept up with the times and looks like the towns you see in the movies where they have a ma and pa general store, police officers with revolvers instead of glocks, and everyone is very religious." James said.

"But doesn't the file says something about a cult? How do they play into all of this?" Mathew asked.

"No clue. I'm sure though we will get some more detailed answers when we arrive." James said.

"I hope they have a smash burger there." Susy said as she grabbed her stomach in hunger.

"I doubt it but I'm sure there is a diner with good food." Mathew said.

"I wonder if the women are cute." James smugly said.

"H-HEY! I'm cute!" Susy shouted.

"Please. You're as cute as band girl from high school with that short hair of yours." James said.

"James, come on. Susy's not that bad looking. I'm sure some lucky guy is gonna sweep her off her feet someday." Mathew said with a wink which got Susy blushing but she hid it by looking out the window.

"Awe, how sweet. Flirting with the ladies again Mathew? Hahaha." James laughed.

"At least I'm better with them than you James." Mathew bragged.

"Whatever man." James said as he went back to concentrating on the road.

As they kept driving for thirty minutes, something strange was happening. The further the three drove, the more the scenery was changing. Trees on either side of the highway went from lush with life to dead and decaying. The road was beginning to change as well from normal to cracked and deteriorated. The three police officers didn't know why all around them seemed lifeless but they tried to ignore it as they kept driving.

"How much longer James?" Susy asked.

"We still have ten miles to go before we are in the next county. Once we pass through, Ghost will be in sight." James said.

"Whatever the case may be…I'm getting a weird vibe." Mathew said.

"Yeah. It's like the closer we are getting to our destination the more devastated everything is looking." Susy said

"Come on guys. It's almost fall so of course everything is looking like its dying. The trees are obviously going to lose some leaves and the roads haven't been maintenance in a while. So it's going to look a little spooky but it's going to be alright." James said trying to convince the others it was going to be alright but mainly he was secretly trying to convince himself.

The three kept driving in silence for another hour. Afterwards, the long trip was finally reaching its end. The tiresome drive for the three was unnerving but got over it as they finally reached their location…Ghost.

Chapter 2

The three police officers arrived to their location the town called Ghost and all three of them felt a strange chill in the air as they took in the scenery…

"This place…seen better days." Susy said as she saw some ruined buildings.

"Yeah it's almost like a real ghost town. Are we supposed to live in this shitty place for a whole week?" James complained.

"Well…Lets just get to the sheriff's office and have a talk with the town's sheriff." Mathew said and all three nodded in agreement as they all got serious about the situation.

As the three drove deeper into town, they saw not only the ruined buildings but homeless people and suspicious citizens in the streets. Everyone was giving the three police officers looks like they shouldn't be here and that's exactly what all three were feeling as they felt the sense of uneasy in this town. However, Mathew was feeling something else as well.

"Sarah came to this place to see her family? What could she be thinking? I hope she's alright…" Mathew thought as he rode along for the ride into this decollate town.

Once the three police officers arrived at the sheriff's office, they all saw the sheriff standing on his front porch smoking a cigarette while holding a pump-action shotgun. The three then got out of the car and walked up to the sheriff…

"Morning. We're from East City." James said.

"This way and call me Cliff." The town's sheriff said as the police officers followed Cliff into the small station.

"I'll get straight to the point. We are needing of more help with our situation." Cliff said.

"What are you talking about?" Mathew asked.

"You remember passing by a group on your way into town right?" Cliff asked and all three nodded.

"…Well they were part of the cult I explained in the report. Their numbers not only grew but now their crimes are getting bolder. I've been putting away more people than I could count but the prison bus only comes but once a week…Now it doesn't come at all since he showed up to this town." Cliff said.

"He?" James asked.

"I don't know his real name but his followers and locals call him Key. He's been making our small cult problem even worse as the people were getting restless and started abducting others." Cliff said and while he was talking, Mathew saw on the wall the people that have gone missing until one particular photo caught his eye…Sarah.

Mathew kept his mouth shut though but still couldn't look away from the photo of his girlfriend. It wasn't until he heard Susy's voice is when he snapped out of his trance.

"Sad, huh?" Susy said as she looked at all the photos as well.

"Y-yeah…We should do something." Mathew said.

"Why haven't you went to the state department about all this going on!?" James demanded.

"We've tried but they didn't believe how serious this was. We've been on our own since this all started. So please…Help me put an end to this." Cliff said with a sincere tone.

"…Can I have a moment with my colleagues?" James asked.

"Sure. I'll just go outside and have a walk." Cliff said as he left the three alone in the station…

"Look…I'm not going to sugarcoat this shit. I think we walked into something a lot bigger than what the lieutenant said." James said.

"I know…but we can't just leave these people. What if there aren't some people involved in this cult? They're innocent and need our service and protection." Susy said.

"Also, what if we can find some of the missing people while helping the town? They need our help even if it's not much." Mathew pointed out.

"Shit…Well I guess there is no backing out of this now, huh? Alright…I'll go find the sheriff and tell him we'll be helping the best way we can. I need you two to go gather Intel about anything. We need to know about the cult, its leader, the victims, and anything that could help us in a peaceful resolution." James said and Mathew nodded along with Susy in agreement.

The three exit the station and went into town on foot so they don't startle some of the townsfolk. James went to find Cliff, Susy went to the diner for information but mainly just to stuff her face, and Mathew went to the town's hall to see if the mayor of the town had some answers…

While walking down streets to find the sheriff, James felt an odd sensation. The street he walked down was quiet…Almost like he was being watched. He looked but no one was around.

"Shit…Where the fuck is that damn Sheriff? CLIFF?" James shouted as he called out for Cliff but nothing answered him back.

Suddenly, as James passed an ally in between two buildings, a bag was thrown over his head from behind. James struggled but was punched in the gut and from the wind being knocked out of him, was hit again but this time in the head. James blacked out and his body was taken away from prying eyes…

Without knowing her colleague's fate, Susy entered the dinner. However, the sight was gruesome as bodies were everywhere. Flies buzzed around the corpses, dried blood stained the restaurant's furniture, and the smell of death hung heavily as Susy looked in horror at what she was seeing…

"W-What is this?! I…I got to go find Mathew and James before…" Susy said as she tried to open the door to leave but for some reason it was locked.

"Going somewhere..." A hooded man said as he came from behind the shadows…

"F-F-FREEZE!" Susy shouted as she pulled out her gun in a panic.

"Ohhh…How cute. Do you think that little toy will do you any good little police bitch?" The man said as he pulled out an aluminum bat.

"Drop the bat! I will shoot!" Susy said but then saw more men come from behind the counter all dressed the same.

"S-STAY BACK!" Susy shouted but all the men smiled as they looked at Susy with sadistic eyes.

"All hail…The demon king…" The men quietly chanted as they slowly advanced.

Susy shoot the first man that was closest but that didn't stop the slow sinister advance of the cultist men. Susy panicked as she shot more but that didn't matter since there were more men than her bullets. After she ran out of ammo, Susy was surrounded by three of the men still alive…

"Didn't I tell you? That little toy will not stop us…" The hooded man said as he grabbed Susy along with the others and she screamed on top of her lungs until her screams were heard from no more…

Later on that evening, Mathew still couldn't find anyone to talk with him. It was like everyone vanished and the mayor couldn't be found once he entered the town hall. In fact, no one could be found and it felt very strange as the emptiness of the town hall was unnerving. However, Mathew decided to look into the town's records to see if they had anything about what was going on.

File after file Mathew searched until he finally gave up because it was just a waste of time since he couldn't find anything. With a sigh, he decided to leave the town hall to find James and Susy to report in. However, the twin wooden doors of the entrance slammed shut in front of Mathew and he heard a laughter from behind him…

"Hahahahaha. Foolish…Just foolish." Cliff said as he revealed himself from the shadows.

"Sheriff? What's going on? Why did these doors shut?" Mathew demanded.

"This is the power the demon king has given us. In return, we help Key find the lock which will unleash Hell and the demon king will bring forth a new age of death and darkness…" Cliff said.

"What the hell are you talking about!? You where the one that called us in to stop this nonsense Cliff! Why are you apart of this cult and who is Key!?" Mathew demanded.

"We were short on supply of souls to offer to the demon king and Key told us he will find the lock once the demon king has enough souls of the dead. So, we called families, friends, and anyone willing enough to travel into Ghost. However, IT STILL WASN'T FUCKING ENOUGH!" Cliff shouted as he shot his shotgun in the air which hit the roof of the town hall but still had it trained on Mathew afterwards so he wouldn't go for his sidearm.

"Cliff… You know this is bullshit, right? There is no demon king and this Key guy has been lying to you. Please just put the shotgun down and we can end this in a civil manner." Mathew said as he held up a hand to calm Cliff down.

"Mathew was it? You know, I made up that report just to get some more souls for our lord and master. However, most neighboring divisions didn't fall for it until your Lieutenant agreed. I was overjoyed we had three more sacrifices. Now…be a good little police boy…and DIE!!" Cliff shouted as he pulled the trigger but Mathew quickly jumped to a nearby desk before getting shot.

"Mathew…No use hiding." Cliff said as he pumped the shotgun and was about to shoot again.

Mathew had his sidearm but this was the first time he might had to use it against someone. For two years he's been a police officer but never had to shoot at someone before. Now as sweat rolled down his face, Mathew flipped off his safety and readied his gun.

"Come out Mathew and drop the gun son. If you do, I'll make sure it will be quick." Cliff said as he stepped forward ever so slowly and Mathew could hear every step being taken.

"What should I do? He has the upper hand. If I come out he'll shoot me…If I say here he'll get close enough to kill me…What should I do!!!?" Mathew thought as he panicked.

Suddenly, Mathew spotted a chair on wheels next to him and got a plan to quickly end this and hopefully no one will have to die. With one swift action, Mathew pushed the chair as hard as he could with his foot and made the chair go flying across the floor. Cliff saw this and shot at the chair. However, before he could rechamber another shell, Mathew came out of hiding and shot next to cliff with his gun.

"Drop it!" Mathew shouted.

"Don't think so kid. The demon king will be summoned and a soul will be given to him even if it's my own." Cliff said as he lifted up his shot gun to fire again but was too late as Mathew shot Cliff in the forehead.

Cliff fell to the ground and blood pooled around his body. Mathew couldn't believe he took a life. However, he had no choice because Cliff would have killed him. Regardless, Mathew regained his focus after a few moments and walked over to Cliff's body.

"I'm…Sorry." Mathew said as he holstered his side arm and grabbed Cliff's shotgun. However, the pump-action shot gun had one shell left in it so Mathew searched Cliff's dead body for more ammo.

"Oh God…" Mathew said at the stench the body was starting to give and he wanted to throw up but used one of his hands to block the smell and continue searching the corpse.

Mathew grabbed three more shells from Cliff's body along with his flashlight since it was starting to get dark outside. Mathew then used one of Cliff's shoelaces to tightly tie the flashlight around the shotgun so he would be able to use the light while holding the shotgun.

"I got to go find James and Susy. If the Sheriff of this town is one of these cultists then we are the only law enforcement here. We need to get out of here and head back to East city to call in the United States Marshals or something…" Mathew said to himself in a panic as he opened the doors of the town hall and left.

However, little does Mathew know, his fellow police officers have been attacked already and Mathew does not know if they are alive in this mess the three found themselves in. The cult along with their leader, Key, are trying to unleash Hell but right now…Mathew feels like they are already in Hell…

Chapter 3

Mathew hugged building after building after what happened in the town hall. Something told him this whole town is a loss and the three should have left when they had the chance. However, time for regrets had past and Mathew kept to the shadows to keep away from detection. The first place closest to him was the diner where Susy said she was going. Mathew prayed she was alright but once he entered the diner he saw the corpses.

"Dear God...What in the hell is going on?" Mathew questioned as he looked at the bodies.

Suddenly, the sun was setting and he was losing day light. Quickly Mathew took off his shirt and pants that were police issued and swapped them with a dead civilian's clothing. He needed to blend in with the populace if he was going to get anything done and save his fellow officers but more importantly, he needed to find Sarah. However, first thing is getting some back up and he needed James and Susy's help with that.

Mathew took off his belt but kept his gun and spare clip just in case. He knew someone was going to find the belt along with his uniform but it's better to leave it than having it on him. However, once he was done putting on the clothing and hat to keep is identity mysterious, a man came in wearing a hoodie and holding an aluminum bat…

"Hey man. What you doing here? We already caught the police bitch." The man said behind Mathew.

"Oh um sorry. I just saw some clothing on the floor from another one of those pigs. We need to find him." Mathew played along not to be suspicious. However, the guy came over to investigate what Mathew said and picked up the clothing to look at.

"You're right…but right now we need to go to the ceremony in Ted's basement. They caught one of those fuckin cops earlier today and plan on doing a sacrificial ritual." The guy said as he opened the door for Mathew.

"Is…Key going to be there?" Mathew asked boldly in order to get some information.

"Key? Are you fucking serious? He doesn't have time to fucking deal with these kind of things. The demon king is near remember? He said so two days ago so he has to find Lock before the lunar eclipse that is going to happen tomorrow night." The guy said.

"Oh…right. Sorry." Mathew lied as he acted like he just forgot.

"Come on man. The ritual is going to start soon in Ted's neighborhood four miles from here. I don't want to miss it." The guy said.

"Right…Let's go." Mathew said as he followed the guy to his truck.

The two got in and drove off. Mathew had Cliff's shotgun and his side arm but didn't tell the guy next to him how he got them. Mathew put the side arm behind him in his pants since he left his belt back at the diner. If he still had his police gear on, it would only be suspicious so he had to look the part of someone that's not a police officer. However, this cover of his is only good as long as no one suspects him. Once someone notices that he isn't part of the cult, then Mathew would be in trouble.

The trip to Ted's neighborhood was a fast one because the guy was flooring it the whole way while blasting loud obnoxious music. Mathew didn't like it but forced himself to act like he was enjoying it as much as the driver because he needed to keep his cover.

"Hey man. I didn't get your name?" The guy asked.

"Oh…I'm Matt. From Billy's street." Mathew lied as he tried to make an alias by shortening his name and used one of the streets he saw along the way as a place he was from.

"Oh nice. I'm glad you're here. I noticed you have the Sheriff's shotgun." The guy said.

"Yeah…I found it from his dead body. I think that pig killed him and ran off like a scared bitch." Mathew said but couldn't believe what came out of his mouth. Normally Mathew didn't use profanity much but he really needed this guy to believe he wasn't an outsider so he could blend in more.

"Probably but we'll find out once we comb through the town after the ritual. We need more sacrifices before tomorrow night. Key is so close to finding Lock but the demon king needs more souls to give him the location of Lock." The guy explained.

"Yeah…" Mathew said pondering who Lock was. It was oblivious that Key was looking for someone he named Lock in order for his followers to believe him but something was telling Mathew he wasn't going to like what's going to happen once they find this person.

Suddenly, the two made it to their location in a neighborhood that was full of crazed people burning trees, throwing rocks and bottles against house windows, and slutty women along with buff tattooed guys playing some sort of music and making out while groping each other.

"This is chaos…I need to find Susy and James quickly. If what this guy says is true, then James must be who they have as a sacrifice for their ritual. I need to work on a plan to get him out before he's killed." Mathew thought as he tried his

best not to look at the crazed citizens razing the neighborhood.

The truck then pulled up to a house which Mathew assumed was Ted's place. Music and partying was going on and Mathew got out with the guy to walk up to the house.

"Mitch! Welcome back bro." Mathew heard another guy call out to the man that was with him.

"Good to be back Frank. I found Matt here snoopin around for that other cop that came to town but I guess he got the slip on us after killing Cliff." Mitch said.

"We'll find that little bitch but for now let's go. Ted is about to start down stairs." Frank said.

"Matt. We're goin down, you comin?" Mitch asked.

"In a sec. I need to hit the head." Mathew lied to get away real quick.

"Alright man. Just don't take too long. Tonight we are going to hear the fucking pig squeal all the way down to Hell!" Mitch said with enthusiasm before leaving with Frank towards the basement.

Mathew then walked to the back of the house to find out if the basement had a back window. Sure enough, it did. However, there was a woman with a machete and smoking a cigarette guarding it. Mathew knew he would have to get her away from the window so he could see what was going on with James…

"H-Hey babe. What you doin behind here?" Mathew greeted in a street slang voice.

"Buzz off. Ted told me to guard this window so no one could interrupt the ritual." The woman said.

"How about you take a break babe and we could…you know." Mathew said as he played a bluff to attract her away from the window.

"Dude. Get the fucking hint. Even if I were in the mood, I only like chicks. So fuck off playboy or else!" The woman threatened which gave Mathew another idea.

"Or else what cunt?" Mathew insulted.

"W-What the fuck you just call me bitch?! I will fuck you up!" The woman said now giving Mathew her full attention and on the offensive.

"I'm too much of a man for you to kill bitch. Why don't you leave this job for a real man." Mathew provoked with some sexism.

"That's it! I'm going to cut your fucking head off!" The woman shouted as Mathew ran off and the woman chased after him.

Quickly, Mathew gave his hat to a nearby guy up front of the house to throw the woman off. Once the woman got up front she saw this guy wearing the same hat thinking it was Mathew and walked up to him from behind. With one swing of her machete, the guy's head was cleaved off. Suddenly, that guy's girlfriend saw this and grabbed a nearby bottle and smashed it against the woman's head.

The fight against the two women then began and everyone cheer as they gathered around to watch it. This gave Mathew the excuse and means to sneak to the back where the window leading to the basement was.

Once Mathew arrived to the window and peered in, he saw James chained up to the wall with three other men in front of him. Two of the men he recognized were Mitch and Frank. The third must have been the homeowner Ted. Suddenly, another guy came in saying something in a panic and the three left to follow that guy. This was Mathew's chance as he quickly opened the window and climbed down into the basement…

"My…God…" Mathew said in horror as he saw James' body. James was shirtless but his chest was covered in blood drenched scars from what Mathew assumed was from a knife. The scars had many unholy symbols on James' flesh along with the words Key and Lock written in many places.

"James! Wake up!" Mathew said as he shook him awake.

"Mmmm…Mathew? Is that…you?" James weakly answered.

"It's me. Let's get you out of here…" Mathew said as he tried to untie James from the wall after placing the shotgun down against the wall.

However, Mathew heard a gunshot being fired outside and someone yelling to cut it out. Mathew assumed it was that Ted guy shouting to end the fighting between the two women. He knew his time was almost up as he hurried to rescue James and get him out.

Mathew untied James and hurried him out the window. However, once he went back to retrieve the shotgun, he heard the door open and the three men came in…

"W-What the fuck!?" Mitch shouted.

Mathew dove for the shotgun and fired it in one quick action. Mitch and Frank caught the blast of the shot but Ted came from behind and pulled out his revolver. He then shot Mathew in the shoulder and was about to shoot again but realized the gun ran out of bullets.

Unable to use both arms at the moment, Mathew pulled his side arm out from behind him with his good arm and fired it at Ted's head killing him. Mathew didn't waste time as he quickly grabbed the shotgun he dropped earlier and threw it out the window along with the handgun.

Mathew then got out himself before someone else came in. James was weak from torture but forced himself to grab the shotgun and hobbled himself along with Mathew into the nearby bushes. The two kept at escaping once they heard behind them men yelling and cars starting.

"We gotta get out of here." Mathew said but then noticed James collapsed from exhaustion.

The pain finally took its toll on James as he was unable to continue but Mathew just put the handgun back in his pants behind him and carried James on his back. However, Mathew had to leave the shotgun since his hands were full from carrying James.

"Mathew…the shotgun." James said weakly.

"Don't worry about that. We need to get out of here before they find us." Mathew said as he hurried to escape.

Mathew hadn't ran this much since his days back at the police academy where they put him through long jogs with the others during training. However, this was the first time he had to actually run away from someone instead of running after them. It couldn't be helped though because he needed to get James and himself to safety.

Once Mathew and James were far enough away from the neighborhood and from the pursuers, they found a shack that seemed abandoned. With limited options, Mathew put James down gently and readied his side arm. Mathew had four rounds in his clip and a full magazine for back up in case he had to reload. However, Mathew knew he would have to conserve his ammunition in case he needed it.

"Mathew…Be careful." James said sitting against the shack.

"I will. Yell if anyone comes." Mathew said as he opened the door and searched the shack for any hostiles.

The shack seemed empty until he saw something move from underneath a pile of rubble. Mathew's heart was racing because he might have to shoot whomever was coming out if they proved too resistant. Suddenly, it was a child that came out and Mathew was relieved. However, the child saw Mathew and got very scared.

"Hey hey hey. Don't be afraid. I'm a police officer." Mathew said as he put away his side arm.

"No…" The child said.

"No what?" Mathew asked in a soft tone.

"You are not a police officer." The child said.

"Oh you mean because my clothing. Sorry I had to change and-" Mathew said until more children all around him came out of hiding.

"What I meant was…You are a sacrifice." The child said with a sadistic grin and all the kids attacked Mathew with sharp objects.

From broken bottles to sharpened sticks and rocks, the children tried to kill Mathew. However, Mathew was strong enough to push some of the children off but was still getting cut and stabbed a few times. Mathew's gun fell out and got kicked to the front door. James saw this and grabbed the gun. With a single shot to the air, the children stopped the assault on Mathew.

"Get the fuck out of here NOW!" James shouted and the children ran away into the forest.

"Are you alright?" James asked seeing Mathew sitting on the ground.

"…No not really. How…Why would kids…" Mathew said completely shocked at what just happened.

"It's this fucking town man. We need to find Susy and get the hell out of here." James said.

The two stayed in the shack for what seemed like an hour so they could tend to their wounds and rest up a little. However, both knew they couldn't stay here for long because the cultists would soon find them once the kids from earlier tell them Mathew and James' location. So the two walked out and headed towards the town again.

It was another mile before the two officers made it back to town and along the way James found a shirt to put on to cover his scars from being tortured. However, once they reached the town they heard yelling from a group of people and a scream that was louder than the yelling. Both Mathew and James knew that voice that was screaming and both said her name at the same time… "Susy!"

Chapter 4

Mathew and James hurried over to where the crowd of people were in the middle of the street. Suddenly, their eyes saw Susy tied up in chains on top of a wood pile against a large wooden pillar.

"Burn the bitch!" A cultist woman shouted.

"Send her to Hell!" A cultist man shouted next.

"Make her suffer!" Another cultist man yelled.

James and Mathew had to do something and now. However, the side arm they had wasn't enough to stop all of the crazed cultists since all of them were not afraid to die. Mathew and James just looked with fear as they saw Susy had her face cut up, her clothing stripped except her underpants and undershirt, and had a black eye from someone hitting her. Suddenly, someone threw a bottle full of rum at Susy's face and she was bleeding as the flammable alcohol was drenching her body.

"James! We need to do something!" Mathew panicked.

"I know! But what can we do? If we start firing they might start the fires!" James said.

"We got no choice! They are about to burn-" Mathew said until someone already lit one of the torches and was ready to burn the wood pile.

"Shit!" Mathew said as he grabbed the handgun ready to stop them until…

"What do we have here?" A man dressed in a dark red robe said as he approached the populace with two others dressed in dark grey robes.

"Who is that?" James whispered.

"Lord Key." The man holding the torch said bowing down to him.

"Looks like we have another sacrifice to the demon king. Very nice…However! I was informed a few hours earlier that the last sacrificial ritual was interrupted by an intruder." Key said.

"B-But my lord…We had nothing to do with that and we-" The man said until his throat was grabbed violently by Key and was lifted off the ground with unbelievable strength.

"SILENCE! Did I ask for fucking excuses!? No! I came to inform you all that delaying the arrival of the demon king is unacceptable! If I find out that one of you had stopped our master's arrival or was unable to prevent interruption with the rituals, then I will personally see that you will suffer a fate worse than death." Key threatened as he snapped the man's neck that he was holding.

Key then threw the corpse on top of the pyre and walked away with his two loyal followers closely behind. James and Mathew couldn't believe what they just witnessed. Key himself looked to be inhuman with impossible strength the likes neither of them had ever seen before.

"Mathew. We need to get out of here, Susy's a goner. We need to escape and come back with backup and the fucking national guard!" James whispered in fear.

"You go but I gotta save Susy." Mathew said.

"Are you out of your damn mind!? Think about this! If those cultists catch you, you'll be next in their twisted rituals! I'm sorry but Susy's a lost cause. Either come with me or I'm leaving you behind. Make your choice…" James said as he waited for Mathew's answer.

Mathew knew James had a good point but he didn't want to leave Susy as Mathew looked back at her. Suddenly, Susy's eyes saw Mathew's and a sense of hope filled her face. After seeing Susy's face, Mathew couldn't leave her…

"I'm saving her. Please James…Will you help me?" Mathew asked.

"Help you? How!? I told you once we try anything, the cult is going to kill us!" James said.

"Not if we quickly execute a plan." Mathew said.

"A plan? What the hell are you talking about?" James asked.

"Just…follow my lead. Once you see an opening, go and get Susy and run away as far as possible." Mathew said handing James the handgun and spare magazine. James nodded in agreement.

"HEY! There's someone sneaking over there! Let's get him!" Mathew shouted as he ran down the street and others saw him and believed him.

Most of the cultists ran to follow Mathew believing his fib but a handful stayed behind. Without waiting for the rest to follow, James pointed the gun towards the remaining cultists.

"Let her go!" James shouted.

"You! You are a sacrifice too! Get him!" A man said as him and the remaining cultist group that didn't run off tried to attack James but James fired the gun over and over again.

James was able to kill the cultists but wished he didn't have to kill them. However, he was given no choice as they all rushed him without any sign of fear. Once he reloaded the gun with the last magazine that Mathew gave him, he rushed over to Susy and freed her from the wood pile.

"James…" Susy said with relief.

"No time! We need to leave now!!" James said as he ran with Susy westbound towards the lumberyard unintentionally which was a mile away. However, on Mathew's end wasn't as easy as he was leading the mob of cultists away…

"This way!" Mathew shouted.

"We've been running for a while and we still haven't seen anyone." A man cultist said.

"Yeah where the hell is this person you've been saying that was sneaking around. Doesn't look like anyone is here!" A woman cultist said.

"He's here! We gotta find him!" Mathew shouted in desperation for the cultists to believe his lie.

"I think this fucker is lying to us!" Another cultist man said.

"Yeah! He doesn't look familiar too. I think he's that cop that came into our town!" Another cultist man said.

"GET HIM!" The first cultist man shouted and the crowd chased after Mathew now.

"Shit!" Mathew yelled in panic as he was now being chased eastbound.

Suddenly, Mathew saw an abandoned high school after running for another ten minutes. He then decided to run into it and try to lose the cult chasing after him. However, once he entered the doors the cult stopped…

"Dumbass." One of the cultist woman said.

"Now he'll be sacrificed to the demon king without us having to do anything. Let's get back to burn that woman cop." A cult man said and the group left the school.

Mathew saw from behind a corner within the school the cult leaving and was ready to leave himself once he knew the coast was clear. However, once Mathew reached the front doors of the school, the doors would not budge…

"What the hell?!" Mathew said as he pushed and pulled but the doors would not open either way.

"Shit! Maybe the cult locked it from the other side." Mathew said as he tried busting the window glass door but the glass didn't break neither.

"What the fuck is this?!" Mathew shouted but then heard a loud scraping noise and turn to see a large figure with a black hood covering its whole head.

In its hand was a large pipe with nails sticking out of it through the whole shaft. The large figure of a man's hand was pierced from these nails and was wrapped over and over again with barbed wire to keep him to hold the pipe. Mathew was frightened as the large man swung the pipe and tried to hit Mathew. However, Mathew did dodge the attack but was beyond scared as he ran for his life down the hallways of the school.

The windows of the school were boarded up and would take Mathew a while to open one but with that huge man chasing after him, escape was impossible right now. With limited options, Mathew ran into a class room to try and barricade himself from this hulking monster that's perusing him…

Meanwhile, Susy and James found the lumberyard and made their way into the site's office trailer. James boarded up the doorway after locking it and Susy did the same with the windows with whatever the two could find to keep the cult at bay if they found them.

"We should be safe here until tomorrow night." James said once the two were secure within the structure.

"What makes you say that? Those cultists will find us eventually! We need to get out before it's too late!" Susy said.

"Not necessarily. When I was being tortured, I overheard the cultist say something about tomorrow night's lunar eclipse. Once that happens, the cultists will find out their plans have failed and turn on their leader. That's when we will escape and get help putting this whole fucking town away for good." James said.

"What happens during this eclipse the cult is working towards?" Susy asked.

"Supposably, we are sacrifices towards their demon king's revival. Their leader, Key, is supposed to find someone called Lock and unleash Hell. Then the demon king will arrive." James explained.

"So…Why do they need to kill us? Shouldn't they kill each other?" Susy asked.

"No clue. Perhaps, the cult is exempt to this rule if they can bring in more people to be sacrificed. Either way, they are crazed criminals. We need to find a way to escape or the very least contact someone in Easy City to send rescue." James said until both his and Susy's eyes fell on a phone in the small office trailer they were in.

Both had high hopes as James walked over to the phone to see if a connection could be made for a phone call. However, once he placed the phone to his ear, the silence told him it was dead as he put the phone back on the hook. Susy knew it was dead without James telling her because his disappointed body language said it all.

Suddenly, the two heard loud yelling from the distance as they saw torches in the dark from the windows. Both knew they had to hide and quickly before the cultists looked inside. However, the handgun that James had only has fifteen rounds within the magazine and the crowd that was coming were dozens of them…

Back at the school, Mathew backed away from the door of the classroom after bracing it with many desks and chairs. However, that wasn't enough resistance as the huge man that was trying to kill him was bashing the door outside of the classroom.

Mathew searched frantically for anything that might help him fight or the very least escape this monster of a man. Suddenly, Mathew realized this was a science room with lab tables that had Bunsen burners on them. Seeing that the classroom furniture wasn't going to last for very long against the door, Mathew rushed to the lab tables.

"I hope this works." Mathew panicked as he turned on all the burners and busted the nozzles so the gas came out faster and in more quantity.

With hope, Mathew then searched for any matches or something that that could ignite a flame. After searching everywhere, Mathew finally found a lighter in the teacher's desk and opened it. However, the gas was in the air thickly and made it hard to breathe.

Suddenly, the crazed giant finally busted through the doors in a rage and rushed in without thinking. Mathew quickly made it out and turned on the lighter once he was clear. The giant turned around once he didn't see his prey but did see the lighter being thrown into the room with him and erupted flames all around him within the classroom.

"Take that you son of a bitch!" Mathew shouted with bravado but was soon terrified once he saw the man walk out covered in flames but turn his head down the hall towards Mathew.

"W-What the hell…" Mathew said in shock but then saw something even more frightening.

The hood masking the man's head burned off fraction by fraction until Mathew saw the man's head revealed. His left eye was missing, the teeth was sharpened to look like daggers, and his skin was not only burned but some of the man's flesh on his face was gone to the point you saw parts of his skull.

"Shit! What the hell is this guy!?" Mathew thought in fear as the man then made his advance.

Mathew didn't waste any time as he ran for his life. The monster behind smacked the lockers with his nailed pipe over and over as he walked angrily. Mathew had to put some distance between him and this freak of nature so he could find a way out. However, Mathew ran aimlessly without knowing the exits of the school.

Suddenly, as he made one corner and stopped in front of door to lean on to catch his breath, the door opened and hands grabbed Mathew from behind to pull him in…

"If you wanna stay alive, shut the fuck up before you scream." The girl's voice said behind Mathew.

"What's going on? Who are you?" Mathew whispered once the girl released her grip on Mathew's mouth and walked over to close the door.

"My name is Tiffany. I'm the last survivor of this school since that beast arrived a year ago." Tiffany said.

"You…survived for over a year?" Mathew asked.

"Yeah…It wasn't easy and many of my classmates died trying to escape." Tiffany said.

"Why can't you escape?" Mathew asked.

"Well…A year ago before that…thing came into this school, a new principle was appointed to the high school. He had these new locks installed on the doors that were supposed to lock out anyone who tried to trespass into the school property without permission. However, the locks did the opposite and locked all of us in." Tiffany explained.

"Why?" Mathew asked.

"…I think it was all a part of some sort of plan. Not soon after, we all heard the principle laughing uncontrollably shouting something about a demon king. Then a huge man busted through my classroom with a large pipe and killed off our class one by one. We all tried to escape but the beast killed us all in the school even the principle with in months of hunting us down." Tiffany said.

"I…I'm sorry." Mathew said.

"We should go before it finds us. Follow me." Tiffany said as she opened a vent inside the room they were in and crawled in. Mathew followed but didn't know where she was taking him...

Back at the lumberyard, James and Susy hid behind a large desk in the office building. Voices outside could be heard as the cultists searched throughout the lumberyard. Susy coward in fear as well as James because they knew if they were discovered, they would have to fight their way out.

"J-James...I'm scared." Susy whispered.

"I know...I'm scared too but we got to wait until they leave." James whispered back.

Suddenly, the doorknob to the office building was being turned. Even though James locked it and boarded it up as best as he could, his heart raced at the possibility the cult might get in.

"This place seems locked." A man outside the office trailer shouted.

"Well they probably aren't here but let's burn down this lumberyard just in case." Another man said.

"Shit! We need to get away and fast." James said.

Suddenly, James saw flames outside and knew the cult started to burn the lumber all around in the lumber yard. Without any other option, James quickly ripped off the boards on one of the windows.

"What are you doing?! If they see us, the cult will kill us!" Susy said.

"I rather fight them off and hopefully escape than burned alive. Come on, help me." James said and Susy helped him rip down the last boards.

With the last board ripped off, James unlocked the window and opened it. With a quick look around to see if the cult had seen them, James then looked towards Susy to tell her his plan.

"Alright Susy listen. I'm going first to make sure it's safe before you come out. Once I tell you it is safe with a wave, come out quietly as possible and keep low. We need to try and sneak past these cultist freaks. Understood?" James asked and Susy nodded.

As James walked over towards the window, he was prepared to leave and hopefully get Susy out at least. However, once his head poked out, a knife stabbed James' eye. Susy screamed as James' body was pulled all the way out of the window and a crazed cult member appeared in the window smiling with blood all over his face and holding the knife with James' eye ball still on the tip.

"Hello hello hello… Found two little piggies, hiding from the big bad wolf. Hahahahahaha!" The cultist said.

"AHHHHHHHH!!!!" Susy screamed as the other cultist surround the trailer with torches in hands.

"Don't worry little pig. We aren't going to blow your house down…but we are going to burn it!" The cultist said in the window as the rest of the cult started fires around the trailer and Susy panicked.

She tired escaping from different windows but cult members were there too. She then tried the front door but as soon as she took off the barricades she and James placed earlier and opened the door, a crowbar stabbed into her gut. Susy then fallen to the floor bleeding fiercely.

Curled up and crying as flames grew and the cult laughed and cheered outside the office trailer, Susy knew she was going to die. James wasn't dead though as he grabbed his face in pain. However, once he became focused on what happened, it was too late. Susy's screams were heard as she was being burned alive and it was loud and more terrifying than anything James ever heard before…

"Well well well. Aren't we a tough one to kill? However, I think it's time you had a proper sacrificial ritual…and I just know the perfect place too." The cult man said with a smile then bashed James' face knocking him out.

"Keep him alive for the ritual and bandage that face of his before he bleeds out." The cult man said and the others did what he said. James' unconscious body was dragged to a van near the lumber yard and the cult drove off…

Meanwhile, back at the school Mathew followed Tiffany through the vent she shown him earlier. However, once they got through the ventilation, Mathew saw the room he entered following Tiffany.

"This looks like the gymnasium." Mathew said looking around.

"Because it is dumbass. God, here I thought grownups were supposed to be smart." Tiffany snidely insulted.

"Does that…thing know how to get here?" Mathew asked.

"Not really but even it did, I set up many obstacles and tripwires to let me know." Tiffany said as she shown Mathew a wall near the bleachers with cans on strings with numbers on them.

"Neat alarm system." Mathew said.

"Well, it's not perfect but it's better than nothing." Tiffany said as she walked behind the bleachers and Mathew followed.

"You…live here?" Mathew asked seeing Tiffany turn on a lamp that was on burner fuel.

Behind the bleachers had many blankets, clothing laid about, food cans, water bottles, and a bunch of books. Mathew pieced together she got the blankets from the nurse's office from the cots, the clothing from other students that didn't need them anymore, food and water from the cafeteria, and the books from the library for entertainment.

"Yeah…Hopefully help will arrive but…I gotta ask. Who are you? I know I should have asked earlier but I had to get you away from the monster before he found me so…Spill." Tiffany said.

"My name is Mathew. I'm a police officer from East City. I came to this town on orders but didn't know the town's problems were this bad." Mathew explained.

"Wait a minute…When you said the town's problems, you mean…it's like this out there too?" Tiffany asked.

"Yeah…Sorry." Mathew said and Tiffany sat down in disbelief on her pile of blankets.

"Here I thought…I hoped someone or anyone will help me escape this place. I…I should of know after a year…No one was coming." Tiffany said as tears flowed down her face.

"Tiffany…I'm sure you'll get out of here. I'll help you and together we will escape this town." Mathew said placing a hand on Tiffany's shoulder.

"It's not just that…My family…If what you are saying is true. My family is probably…" Tiffany said as more tears watered.

"Hey, don't think like that. You don't know if they escaped or not. They are probably safe and escaped before it was too late." Mathew said to comfort Tiffany and luckily it did as she hugged Mathew in gratitude.

"Thank you…I believe you could be right. Since my dad is the Sheriff." Tiffany said and made Mathew's heart sink like never before…

Chapter 5

Hours pasted during the night and soon came day break. Last night was the most horrifying night of Mathew's life after everything he had went through with his fellow police officers. His girlfriend going missing, a crazed cult was after him, and now he's stuck inside the town's high school with a monstrous man trying to kill him. However, when dawn broke and light hit his face Mathew woke up.

"Mmm...Fuck. Here I thought it all was just a damn nightmare." Mathew said but then realized Tiffany was gone.

"Great..." Mathew said not knowing where the girl had ran off to.

However, that was not the only thing plaguing Mathew's mind. He knew he would have to break the news to Tiffany eventually about her father's death but that was easier said than done. Especially since Mathew was the one that killed her father because her father was a part of the cult.

Suddenly, Mathew heard the gate to the vent opened and he quickly got a nearby piece of wood for protection thinking he would have to fight if it was the monster. However, it was Tiffany that came through the vent and Mathew was relieved.

"Morning sleepy head. I got us breakfast." Tiffany said holding up a bag full of fruit cups.

Mathew and Tiffany ate in silence for what seemed like a half an hour and it felt a little awkward. So Mathew decided to break the silence with discussion of escape…

"So…I noticed the windows of the school were boarded up. Do you think we can break one open and escape?" Mathew asked.

"I've tried but it was that monster that boarded them up and he made sure those boards were firmly secured with many nails. Even if we could get them off, the noise will alert the monster and he will come after us." Tiffany said.

"What about the doors? If there is no electricity in the school, how come they are electronically locked like that when I came in?" Mathew asked.

"To be honest I'm not quite sure…However, I think it's because there are backup generators down in the basement of the school but that's where that thing lives. I've seen him dragging the dead bodies of the students and teachers down there and…I think he eats them." Tiffany said now putting down her fruit cup after losing her appetite.

"So…If we can distract the monster. One of us can go down there and turn off the generators." Mathew said.

"Distract him?! Are you crazy?" Tiffany asked.

"Well it's our best option. Besides, you can't live here for the rest of your life Tiffany. You have to live your life without having to watch your back." Mathew said.

"Yeah...but..." Tiffany said now shaking nervously.

"Hey...It will be alright. I'll take the hard job of distracting this monster. You know this school like the back of your hand so I'll let you go down to turn off the generators but make sure to rip out the cords or cut them. That way the power can't come back even if that thing tries to turn it back on." Mathew said.

"But...How can you distract him? If he gets a hold of you, you'll..." Tiffany said in fear.

"Don't worry. If I die, you can still make your escape." Mathew said.

"Do...Do you think...I'll find my father again?" Tiffany asked.

"...I'm sure you'll find him." Mathew said trying to hold back the guilt within his conscious.

"Alright…If we are really doing this, we need to plan it out." Tiffany said as she looked through her things for something.

"What are you looking for?" Mathew asked but then saw Tiffany pull out a map and a Taser that was as small as a lipstick tube.

"Here. The entrance to the basement is on the other side of the school so I'll have to run as fast as I can. Take this Taser my dad gave me. It only has enough charge for one attack so use it wisely." Tiffany said as she shown Mathew the map and gave him her Taser.

"Why did your father give you this?" Mathew asked.

"Well...My dad just wanted me to defend myself in case someone tries to hurt me but right now I believe it would be in better use if you had it." Tiffany said.

"I don't know if it will take that monster down but thank you. I'm sure it will come in handy just in case." Mathew said as he put it in his pocket.

"Now. The way I see it, this hall way that is near the basement has an emergency exit. Once the power from the generators is turned off, I'll run out but you need to find a way out also." Tiffany pointed out.

"Don't worry I will but you should run away as fast as you can once you are out. Don't wait for me because if that thing kills me, it will come after you." Mathew warned.

"But…Where should I go?" Tiffany asked.

"Anywhere than here but if you can, try heading to the nearest town and call authorities. Someone has to stop this craziness going on in this town." Mathew said and Tiffany nodded…

Meanwhile in a large mansion on the other side of the town. James woke up in a cage in what seemed like the basement but it looked like a dungeon. His face was wrapped up on the right side where he lost his eye. However, his left still saw where he was and it was gruesome.

"W-What the fuck!? WHERE THE HELL AM I!!!?" James screamed as he saw in terror bodies of dead women strung up in chains from the ceiling. The chains pieced their flesh and their eyes looked black like something had possessed them.

"They…were failures." Key said as he appeared from the shadows.

"Y-You! You are the cult leader!" James panicked as he backed away from him but he couldn't go any further since his back was against the cage.

"Yes…I'm Key. The one who will bring Hell to this earth with the revival of the demon king." Key said grabbing the bars of the cage.

James couldn't believe his eyes. Up close, Key's face looked barely human. His eyes were glowing yellow, his teeth were unnaturally curved, and his smile…looked demonic.

"I…I-I don't understand. How are you going to bring Hell?" James asked nervously.

"By finding Lock. She is the one who will open the doorway for the demon king. The ones above you…were failed candidates. They offered themselves to me but none of them could become Lock!" Key shouted as he yanked on the bars of the cage and ripped it open.

"Do you know…There is only one way to find Lock…?" Key asked.

"N-No…" James nervously said as he could feel the evil from Key. He knew the answer but didn't want to anger Key so he played dumb as best as he could in order to live.

"By killing and sacrificing others will bring forth the location of Lock. The cult sees to that and the demon king will grant me the knowledge of the whereabouts of Lock." Key said.

"S-So are you going…to s-sacrifice me?" James asked now trembling as sweat rolled down his face.

"No no…but you do something for me, I'll make sure you can leave this place alive." Key said tracing his dark nailed finger slowly down James' face.

"D-D-Do what?" James asked fearfully at what Key wants him to do.

"Find your little cop friend that you came here with…and kill him." Key said.

"M-Mathew?! I-I can't kill him! He's my friend!" James said.

"Oh don't worry…You'll soon do what I want and he's going to make sure of it." Key said as he backed away and then one of Key's loyalists from earlier wearing the grey robe came into the cage.

"Well James…I'm glad to see you again." The mysterious man said.

"That voice…Who are you!?" James demanded until he saw the man reveal his identity.

"No…Not you too…Lieutenant Marcus!" James shouted after seeing his Lieutenant from the East City Police Department.

"Yes…Why did you think I decided to send you three here in the first place? The demon king's revival is nearly at hand and Lord Key will bring him forth once Lock is found." Marcus said.

"H-How could you? YOU BASTARD!! WE TRUSTED YOU!" James screamed.

"Exactly. It was perfect. I wished I could have sent the whole force over but that would have been problematic. So I decided to send a small team. It wasn't much but it's an offering to ensure my place with Lord Key in the demon king's new kingdom!" Marcus said.

"I…I"LL KILL YOU!" James shouted as he charged at Marcus but was stabbed in the neck swiftly with a syringe and mysterious green liquid quickly entered James' blood stream.

Suddenly, James fell to the floor of the cage and couldn't move his limbs. However, he was still fully conscious and his eyes were trained on Marcus and Key looking down on him with dark smiles.

"Don't worry James. You will do as told and we are going to show you how." Marcus said as he grabbed James…

Back at the school, Mathew ran down many hallways until he heard crunching noises a few yards away. Suddenly, Mathew's eyes saw the monstrous man ripping off the flesh of a leg from a body with his teeth. Mathew was about to run but then got an idea since the monster didn't realize him yet.

If he could sneak up on the monster before it noticed, Mathew could use the Taser Tiffany gave him to zap the monster's head and hopefully knock him out at least. Then he could escape once the power that was keeping the doors locked was gone.

With each terrified step, Mathew could hear the monster ripping and chewing the flesh of the corpse. The smell of death and blood hung heavily in the air as Mathew breathed. Once he was a few more feet away from the beast, Mathew accidently stepped on a pair of broken glasses and alerted the monster.

Suddenly, with a deep growl that didn't sound human, the beast got up and turned his attention towards Mathew. Mathew's element of surprise was now gone and he had no choice but to run. However, he made sure where ever he went was far away from the basement staircase so Tiffany could turn off the generators…

Meanwhile, back at the mansion where James was, sounds of screams could be heard in its dungeon. James was strapped to a metal chair while Marcus tortured James with many tools.

"How many does that make it? James?! ANSWER ME!?" Marcus shouted as he applied a soldering iron to James' face.

James screamed in pain as the soldering iron went up his face very slowly towards where he lost his eye last night. Ever since James was strapped to this chair, it felt like hours of unrelenting pain to him. James' sanity was on the edge of breaking as Marcus demanded James to keep track of how many times he got tortured.

"F-Fifty s-seven." James weakly said in pain as he shook from being tortured.

"Good. I'm glad you are keeping count James. Now…Will you do as Lord Key asked?" Marcus asked.

"N-n-no!" James screamed as blood was dripping down his face.

"Alright then. I guess it's time to use Mr. Clippers again." Marcus said as he pulled out his wire cutters he had used on James earlier.

"NO NO! PLEASE STOP!!" James begged but fell on deaf ears…

Back within the school, Mathew was running as the monster kept on swinging his nailed pipe to try and kill him. However, Mathew was nibble enough to duck and dodge his attacks and finally busted through two doors and found himself within the Cafeteria.

"ROOAARR!" The monster screamed as it charged inside too but when it did, he couldn't find his prey.

Mathew hid behind tables that were turned on their sides. However, when he glanced a peek to see if the monster had found him or not, he saw the monster was searching by flipping tables and chairs.

"Shit…What can I do to fucking stop this thing!?" I can't risk revealing myself but if I ignore him for too long, he might leave towards the basement and find Tiffany. What should I do?!" Mathew thought as he began to panic but then saw something across the way.

On the other side of the counter was a very large cutting table the lunch ladies must have used to cut large foods into fractions like with pizza or breads. Attached to the table was a very large blade that was on a hinge.

Mathew had a plan to at least disable the monster before he left the cafeteria but then saw he was nearing the door and Mathew had no choice now. With a loud yell, Mathew charged and then used the Taser he had to zap the monster with the whole charge.

It wasn't enough though but it did make the monster drop his weapon. However, the monster bashed Mathew's arm with a heavy hit which he could have sworn he felt something broke.

"AH!!!!" Mathew yelled in pain.

"ROARRRRRRR!!!!!!" The monster yelled as he was about to attack again.

However, Mathew used his good arm to grab the nailed pipe and smack the monster in the head. Stunned, the monster wobbled around with the nailed pipe stuck in his head. Mathew forgot all about his pain as he charged the monster with all his strength. Mathew pushed him over the counter and the monster fell to the floor.

When the monster was getting back up, he used the cutting table as leverage to get back up. However, Mathew quickly slammed the monster's head by the pipe that was still stuck and pinned him into position with the blade. Mathew slammed the cutting board blade over and over again on the monster's head.

"Die! Die! Just FUCKING DIE!!!!!" Mathew screamed as blood, flesh, and parts of the monster's face was flying everywhere.

After Mathew killed the monster man of the school, he fell to the ground breathing heavily. This was unbelievably tough for him but he managed to kill the beast. Suddenly, Mathew heard a loud noise and assumed was the electronic locks shutting down. Mathew then grabbed the pipe the monster had and walked out of the school through a nearby exit…

Earlier back at the mansion, James' torcher was continuing…

"James? How many times was it now?" Marcus cheerfully asked.

"O-One…h-hund-dred a-a-and s-seventy t-two…" James struggled to say as blood was coming from his eyes, ears, mouth, nose, and his open eye hole.

"Pain will stop once you decide to kill Mathew James…" Marcus said with a smile.

"K-Kill…" James said.

"Yes James…Kill." Marcus said.

"Kill…Kill….KILL!" James shouted as his sanity was now gone and all he could think of was killing.

"Very good James. Now take this knife and go kill Mathew." Marcus said as he released James' restraints but James then sliced Marcus' eyes with a quick motion. With a sharp yell, Marcus grabbed his face in anguish.

"KILL KILL KILL! KILL ALL!!!" James shouted as he stabbed Marcus to the ground over and over again until he was dead.

James then got back up from the ground. His crazed eyes saw the staircase with a sadistic smile, James walked up the stairs laughing. He eventually got back up to the mansion's main hall. There was the entrance and James walked out, knife in hand and dripping with blood…

Back at the school, Mathew finally found an exit. It was good to finally get out of the school. Even if it was just the rest of last night and this morning, it felt longer than it was. Once Mathew exited the school, the midday sun hit his face and it blinded him for a second. However, once his sight returned he saw Tiffany coming up to him…

"Mathew! Are you okay?" Tiffany asked.

"Yeah. I'll be fine. You should have left though like I asked you to." Mathew said.

"I know but I had to make sure you got out and-" Tiffany said until Mathew saw a blade came through her neck from the back and sliced outward.

Blood sprayed like a fountain as Tiffany fell dead to the ground. Mathew saw in horror but what really terrified him was the man whom held the blade and was laughing right now…James.

Chapter 6

James laughed uncontrollably as Tiffany's blood sprayed all over his face before she fell to the ground. Mathew was terrified at what he was witnessing. James killed someone and wasn't himself. Mathew didn't know what was going on but he did know he needed some answers…

"J-James!? What the hell are you doing?!" Mathew yelled over James' laughter to make him stop.

"Kill…Kill…KILL THEM ALL!" James shouted with a sadistic smile.

"She wasn't a cultist James! How could you kill someone that was innocent?!" Mathew shouted but wasn't getting through to him. James then charged madly at Mathew.

"KILL KILL KILL KILL!" James yelled in glee as he swung the knife over and over again to try and kill Mathew.

Mathew dodged James' attacks as best as he could but his injuries from fighting the school monster took its toll and was slowing Mathew's movements. With few options, Mathew tried to fight back with the nailed pipe he took from the monster earlier.

"JAMES STOP!!" Mathew shouted as he tried to defend himself but James thrusted his blade and cut Mathew's hand making him drop the nailed pipe.

Mathew then bolted away from James as fast as he could but James was in pursuit. Mathew then broke into a convenience store that was abandoned and used a nearby metal bar to block the door from opening. However, even though the bar was barricading the door, Mathew knew it wouldn't take James long to figure out another way into the store. Mathew quickly looked for another way out but suddenly heard the back door open and man called out to him…

"This way quickly!" The man said.

With little choice, Mathew did what the man said and followed him through the back door and down an ally. The mysterious man led Mathew into another building after running away from James. Once the coast was clear and it was obvious that they had lost James, Mathew saw what building they were in.

"This looks like a museum…" Mathew said looking around.

"Yes. I've been hiding in here for over a year. Thankfully, none of the cultists know I've been in here." The mysterious man said.

"I don't mean to be rude sir, but who are you?" Mathew asked.

"Oh apologies young man. My name is Harold Jedidiah Ghost. Mayor of the town of Ghost and sixth generation to the Ghost founding family." Harold said.

"You're the mayor? I would have thought you were a part of the cult or the very least sacrificed to their twisted religion." Mathew said.

"No no. I've been in hiding ever since the cult turn the town against me and began massacring the town. First it was the town's hall, then the businesses, then finally and most unfortunately…our school. I was powerless and I cowardly exiled myself to this old museum." The man said in depression.

"I don't think you are a coward sir. You saved my life from…that guy." Mathew said trying to hide the fact James used to be his fellow police officer.

"Well I had to do something. You obviously didn't look like a part of the cult and I never saw you here before. So when I went into town to find some food before the cult came back, I saw you and had to do something before that crazed man killed you." Harold said.

"Thank you sir but I got to ask. Why didn't you seek help before this all went to hell? Neighboring counties could have helped. Heck I'm sure the US Marshals would have stepped in if the situation was dire." Mathew said.

"Yes. I did try to reach out but the cult found out and stopped me before it was too late. They killed my staff and fellow citizens that didn't want anything to do with the cult. However, none of that mattered to the cult as they butchered the whole town week after week for the whole year…" Harold said depressed again by the memories.

"I'm sorry sir…" Mathew said feeling bad for Harold.

"It's alright son but please tell me. Who are you and why are you here?" Harold asked changing the subject.

"I'm a police officer from East City. I've been sent here by request from your town's sheriff along with two other officers. However, once we got here, all hell broke loose and we've been fighting for our lives since yesterday." Mathew explained.

"I'm sorry to hear that. What happened to the other officers?" Harold asked but was met with silence from Mathew.

"…I'm sorry son." Harold said placing a hand on Mathew's shoulder.

"Thank you sir. I hope to get word out about this place. Is there a phone I could use?" Mathew asked.

"I wish. Like I said, the cult stopped my attempt to get help myself by destroying the phone towers and landlines in the area. Even the post office was out of my reach since the cult took over." Harold explained.

"Damn it…" Mathew said now walking over to a nearby bench to sit down.

"You must be tired. Stay here son while I go and get you something to drink." Harold said as he walked away.

"What am I doing here? Why did James try to attack me? Where the hell is Susy? I need to find out something..." Mathew thought as he rested.

Mathew's arm was in pain from earlier but was still able to move it. He was afraid he broke it when fighting that monster in the school but it seemed to be ok. However, he knew he should take it easy for right now before he decided to leave. Mainly because James could still be out there trying to kill him along with the cult as well. So for now, Mathew decided to lay low until later on. However, in the back of the museum, Harold was on a radio that was given to him…by Key.

"H-Hello? Lord Key?" Harold said in the radio.

"What is it, you trash? I thought I told you only to call unless you have a sacrifice for the cult." Key answered.

"Y-Yes my lord. That cop that came to town is here and I-I thought I should let you know." Harold said.

"Very well. However, one of my two subordinates was killed in failing to turn one of those East City police officers so I cannot personally come. However, I'll send some of the cult members to pick up the other one for sacrifice. Keep him there until they arrive!" Key demanded.

"Y-yes my lord…After they take him…Will I see my daughter Eliza again?" Harold asked.

"You have some gall to request that of me little mayor. However, it was you that gave your daughter to me in exchange to stay alive until the day of reckoning. So no, you won't get to see your daughter. In fact she's going to be the next one for the Lock test." Key said.

"But she's only seventeen! You told me Lock had to be eighteen or older for the test to work!" Harold panicked.

"Yes but today is her birthday after all or did you forget?" Key said which terrified Harold because Key was right.

"D-Dear God… P-Please Lord Key…Don't do this! She's my everything!" Harold yelled as tears rolled down his face.

"I will do this in the name of the demon king! It's almost perfect! She turns eighteen on the day the lunar eclipse is supposed to happen and she is the latest generation to the Ghost name? It's like she was supposed to be Lock all along and I didn't even realize it until now!" Key shouted with enthusiasm.

"Y-You…Monster…" Harold said as he listened to Key's maniacal laughter on the other end of the radio.

Suddenly, the transmission was cut off and Harold knew that things had turned for the worse. Dropping the radio, he wiped away his tears and breathed heavily in shock about what's going to happen. Once he calmed down enough, Harold knew what he had to do…

"I got to go tell Mathew to save my daughter and-" Harold said as he turned around to go back to Mathew. However, his chest was stabbed from James' knife…

"Kill the old man…KILL EVERYONE!" James shouted with joy as blood poured from the knife down his arm.

"W-Who are y-you…?" Harold said but died shortly after.

"Dead man said Mathew was here. Kill Mathew…go home…Kill Mathew…go home…Kill Mathew…kill home! HAHAHAHAHAHA!!!" James psychotically laughed.

Mathew was still sitting on the bench until he heard laughter and a chill went down his spine because he knew who it was. The very man that plagued is thoughts recently and the same man who is trying to kill him for and unknown reason too…James.

"Mathewww…Come out to dieee…" James called out while walking towards his direction.

Quickly, Mathew made his way to another part of the museum before James could find him. However, James' footsteps could be heard and Mathew was panicking to find something to defend himself.

Suddenly, Mathew saw he was in a civil war exhibit of the museum and quickly hid before James could find him. Once James arrived, Mathew saw the crazed bloodlust in his face from behind barricade replica of the civil war exhibit. James saw the dummies of civil war soldiers and went on a rampage even though they weren't real.

"KILL KILL KILL!" James shouted as he was smashing many mannequins.

Mathew took this time to quietly sneak his way from cover to cover in hopes to slip past James. However, James saw him once his gaze was near his position and stopped his mindless attack on the exhibit's dummies.

"Mathew…I finally found you." James said with a sadistic grin as he cracked his neck sideways.

"James! What the fuck is wrong with you!? Why are you like this? Where is Susy?! ANSWER ME!" Mathew demanded.

"S-Susy?..." James said until her image flashed in his head and he grabbed it in pain after remembering the screams she made last night from being burned alive.

"AHHH!!!!! SUSY!!!!!" James shouted as he swung his knife around aimlessly like a mad man with tears fiercely flowing down his face.

In the confusion, Mathew saw a broken piece of glass on the ground and in the middle of James' episode, he grabbed the glass. Mathew charged and shoved the sharp shard into James' throat which made him bleed. Then Mathew uppercut James' jaw.

In pain, James had fallen to the ground grabbing his mouth with both hands. Without a second thought, Mathew grabbed the knife and thrusted it over and over again in James' face until his body quit moving.

Tears then dripped down Mathew's face because he had no choice but to put down his friend. However, even though he was in pain, this was no time to wallow in sadness as Mathew picked up the knife and walked out of the exhibit.

"Mayor? Where are you?" Mathew called as he walked to the back of the museum. He then found Harold's body on the floor after walking into a back room…

"Sorry Harold… I promise to make sure they pay for what they did. This has become more than any of us had thought and I don't care what it takes…This will be put to an end." Mathew said.

Suddenly, Mathew heard the front door of the museum being open and multiple people walking in. From the sounds of it, Mathew guessed it was at least a dozen cultists. Yes he was ready to kill them but he wasn't dumb enough to take them on with only a knife. So Mathew decided to retreat for now and made his way out of the back exit.

Meanwhile back at the mansion on the other side of the town, Key walked into a room that had pink wallpaper, boy-band posters, and a big bed with the mayor's daughter chained to the bed frame…

"Eliza Ghost. Nice to see you again." Key greeted with a sinister tone.

"What do you want!?" Eliza spat while looking at Key with hateful eyes.

"I just got done having a chat with your dear old father. He begged for your release but sadly he won't be seeing you ever again." Key said.

"Is…he dead?" Eliza asked.

"Well as soon as he delivers that cop for a sacrifice, he will be. I offered him an exchange for him to keep his life and all he would have to do is give me sacrifices. However, since he lacked in his end of the fucking bargain, I decided to cancel the agreement but that's not what I meant by he'll never see you again…" Key said now looking out the window of Eliza's room.

"W-What do you mean?" Eliza asked now getting nervous with fear.

"You are going to be a part of a very special test tonight. We are going to see if you are worth of becoming Lock." Key said with a grin.

"Wh-What are you talking about? I'm not Lock! You said I was just a hostage so my father wouldn't go to the authorities outside the county!" Eliza said.

"Yes but I'm pressed for time and seeing how you seem to be the most likely, we will test you to find out but it's not going to be pretty. My loyal follower, Rose, will find out for me if you are Lock and then you will be offered to me." Key said with a creepy smile as his eyes looked at Eliza with desire.

"What will happen then?" Eliza panicked but got even more scared as Key got in real close to her ear.

"If you are Lock, then the demon king will be revived into this world…with your heart touched by me." Key whispered into Eliza's ear and sent terrifying shivers down her spine.

"Now…Rose will be in shortly. Behave yourself while I prepare." Key said as he took his leave.

Eliza didn't want to be Key's Lock and she knew she had to get out and quickly because whether or not she was Lock, Eliza was going to die. So Eliza yanked on her chains on the bed post as hard as she could but they wouldn't budge. Suddenly, a grey robbed woman came in with her hood over her eyes. However, a sadistic smile came on Rose's face and fear filled Eliza's soul…

Meanwhile, Mathew went back into town to try to find some weapons, find Susy, and find Sarah.

Luckily, the cult wasn't anywhere to be seen. However, he knew if he was to go after Key, he would need to arm up first.

Mathew headed into the local pawn shop to find anything to help him fight the cult. However, once inside, Mathew saw the place had been ransacked and looted. Not much remained as he searched what he could through the debris.

"Damn it…There has to be something." Mathew said to himself as he searched.

Suddenly, Mathew saw what looked like an old hatchet and some climbing rope. With little choice, he took them but really hopped for a gun but knew that the cult probably had all the firearms. Regardless, Mathew was glad enough that he found something.

Placing the knife in his back pocket, the rope in his other back pocket, and the hatchet in his hand, Mathew made his way out of the pawn shop. There was only one place he could go to find some sort of firearm and that was with the cult hangouts...

Mathew then headed westbound towards the residential areas but had to go through the local lumberyard. However, once he made it to the lumberyard, Mathew saw nothing but charred remains of everything there.

"My god. Looks like they burned the place down." Mathew said as he walked into the lumber yard.

Suddenly, he came upon a burned body but soon realized who it was...

"S-Susy?!" Mathew said as he fell to the ground in disbelief.

"Damn it...DAMN IT ALL!!!!" Mathew screamed in a tearful rage.

After a few minutes of calming down from being upset, Mathew got back up. He hated that everyone that was close to him had died. After Tiffany got killed, after killing James, after seeing Harold dead, and now after discovering Susy…Mathew fell into despair.

"I…I can't believe this is happening…" Mathew said as he began to walk away. However, his despair turned into hatred…a deep and frightening hatred that was fueled by Mathew's need for vengeance…

Chapter 7

Mathew took the time to bury Susy in sadness. However, even though Mathew was grieving, he wanted the cult dead for everything they had done to Mathew and his friends. Once Susy was buried, Mathew moved on towards the residential properties that were a few more miles west from the lumber yard.

After another hour of walking Mathew finally found a cult infested neighborhood. He still had his disguise but word had gotten out to the cult that he was still alive and the cult was gearing up household by household.

Key had demanded the cult to search for Mathew but Mathew only assumed that was what's going on as he saw trucks and cars being loaded up. Mathew couldn't believe the people were doing all this just to find him because it seemed like overkill. However, the cult was a large group of crazed citizens willing to do anything for their demon king's revival.

Mathew hid behind a house and watched the neighborhood empty out little by little until he felt confident enough to venture out and into someone's home to find some sort of gun with some ammunition hopefully. Luckily, the house he hid behind had a back door and Mathew quickly picked the lock as best as he could with the knife he had.

"Come on you piece of shit!" Mathew said then suddenly, a guy came around and saw him trying to break in.

"Hey! Wait a minute you're that-" The guy said until Mathew quickly, shanked the man in the neck and held his mouth with the other hand until the cult member died.

"That was close…" Mathew said as he went back to picking the lock.

Even though he's a police officer, Mathew didn't care about following the law right now because the cult along with its leader are dangerous criminals. So right now, Mathew just cares about finding out where Sarah is and get her out of this town before things get worse.

Suddenly, Mathew heard the door click and knew he had unlocked the back of the house. Quickly and quietly, Mathew grabbed the dead cultist body and dragged him inside and away from sight. Once Mathew got the body inside, he then locked the door and moved a heavy shelf in front so on one could get in.

"Now…Time for me to find something to use." Mathew said to himself as he walked further in the house.

As he searched the house, he managed to find some first aid to treat his wounds he got so far. He was in pain but ignored it as best as he could so he can find Sarah and get out of this town. Sure he was furiously enraged at the cult for killing his friends and the innocent people of Ghost but he knew he couldn't take them all on himself. So for now, Mathew just needed to find Sarah and leave.

After what seemed like an hour of thoroughly searching the house, Mathew gave up finding anything weapon worthy. Suddenly, he thought about that guy he killed before entering the house and went back to his body to see if he had anything on him…

"What's this?" Mathew said as he pulled out a folded up piece paper from the dead body's pocket.

On the paper revealed to be a map of sorts. On this map, it shown a house on the other side of town. This residence was circled in red ink and on the side said: Abandoned veteran's house. Do not enter!!...

"Do not enter? Is this a warning? What's in this house even the cult is afraid of? Whatever the case might be, a veteran's house is sure to have a firearm or two inside. I better check it out." Mathew thought as he left the house he was in from the way he came.

Meanwhile, back at the mansion where Eliza was being held. Rose had Eliza strapped to a chair after getting her out of the bedroom and into the next room over. Eliza struggled but knew it was pointless because she couldn't move from the chair even with all her strength.

"Why struggle young lady? It's only going to get worse if you resist." Rose said.

"Why are you doing this!? Just let me go!" Eliza said as tears rolled down her face.

"I do this for my lord…and my love." Rose said.

"Your…love?" Eliza questioned.

"Yes. My heart belongs to him but he doesn't see me worthy of being Lock since I'm not pure like you." Rose said.

"Pure? Are you talking about…" Eliza began to say.

"Yes. Virgin blood is the first step in being Lock. However, I'm not pure so I handle the tests to find out. Like I said… This is the first step!" Rose said as she stabbed a syringe in Eliza and began extracting blood.

"Ah! That hurts!" Eliza painfully said in discomfort but Rose did not care as she drained a good portion of Eliza's blood.

"Just be a good little bitch and stay here while I go have a look at this. I'll be right back." Rose said after she was done taking Eliza's blood and left her in the chair a little light headed.

Meanwhile, Mathew finally found the old house the map had shown him after searching for an hour. However, the building itself gave a weird vibe like he shouldn't be here…

"This place gives me chills…but I have to go in there. If there is a firearm, I'll be well protected in my search for Sarah." Mathew said as he entered the property unaware of what might be inside.

Again, Mathew used his knife to unlock the door but this time it was a lot quicker. Once the door opened he got hit with a disgusting smell like something or someone had died in the house for quite some time. While grabbing his hatchet tightly in case someone inside might attack him, Mathew entered the house.

"H-Hello? Anyone home?" Mathew called out as he entered. However, once he was a few feet away from the front door, the door slammed shut.

"W-What the fuck!?" Mathew panicked but then heard faint footsteps coming from upstairs.

Mathew didn't know what was going on or how the door slammed shut but someone was here and he needed to confront whomever it was. If this person is a part of the cult, Mathew might have no choice but to kill him. However, if this person was an innocent civilian trying to hide from the cult, Mathew might need to show he's not a part of the cult in case he or she tries to attack him.

"I have no choice but to head up. I got to be careful though and take this slow." Mathew thought as he slowly made his way up the wooden staircase of the old house.

With each step Mathew took, it made a loud creaking sound which made Mathew's nerves tense up even more. Inside the house felt colder with each second Mathew advanced up the stairs. His hand tightly gripping the hatchet and Mathew breathed in the air heavily. He didn't know why but he was getting very nervous as he reached the top of the stairs afraid of what he might find. Suddenly, as he reached the top and looked down the hallway…nothing.

"Whew…For a second I thought-" Mathew said until…

"Hello." A little girl said behind him but when Mathew turned to face this little girl…her eyes were bleeding black as her face smiled.

Without warning and invisible force pushed Mathew hard down the hallway. Mathew was on the floor but when he looked down the hall the lights flickered on and off as the girl slowly walked towards him.

"Will you play with me?" The girl said as her sweet innocent voice turned into a dark sound which made Mathew even more terrified.

Suddenly, the lights went out again but this time she was gone. Mathew quickly got up and looked around in a panic…

"What the fuck! What the hell was that?!" Mathew said as he quickly went back down stairs but when he got to the bottom step…

"You…got to be…fucking kidding me!" Mathew said in disbelief as saw the door was gone and nothing but a wall was in front of him.

"Hehehehehehe. Like that funny man? Welcome to my game. Play nice." The girl's voice said inside the house but Mathew couldn't see her anywhere.

"What is this!? What the fucking hell is going on!?" Mathew shouted as he panicked more.

Mathew then went further into the house unknowing of what to expect next. However, he knew he had to get out. Finding a gun in this place is insane and now he realized why the cult didn't want to enter this place. Mathew was never a strong believer in the paranormal but after what he had just seen, this was a first for him.

Mathew then entered what appeared to be the kitchen but the place was filthy as cobwebs were all over the place, maggots and gnats swarmed the sink and counters, and a new repulsive smell hit Mathew's nose which made him vomit.

"Oh God…" Mathew said after he collected himself.

Suddenly, Mathew saw another door which lead to another room. However, when he opened the door, the room he was in was unholy beyond words. What used to be the living room, now had demonic symbols written on the walls along with the ceiling in massive amounts of dried blood.

"…Jesus…What did I just walk into?" Mathew said as he looked in horror. Suddenly, the room erupted in flames and Mathew quickly ran through the living room and into another door.

After Mathew went through the door and closed it quickly behind him, what he saw next confused him even further. In front of Mathew was a huge maze and he only knew it was a maze because of the pedestal in front of him that had a message on it.

"How the hell is this in a house?" Mathew said in disbelief as he read the message.

The message on the pedestal reads: "If you want out of this place, you must go through my maze. However, this labyrinth will try to kill you if you are not careful. Remember…Your feet walk on false ground but your eyes will lead you astray. Find the hidden room to live this day."

"Find the hidden room? In this place? All I want is out! I should have never walked through that door! Now Sarah might be lost to me forever and I might never get out alive!!" Mathew yelled in stress but calmed down once he sat down in need of a break.

"Calm down. I gotta work this thing out if I'm going to survive this. Now…the message said my feet walk on false ground. Does that mean there is a secret passage somewhere on the ground in this maze? If so, I gotta find it. It might be a way out!" Mathew thought as he got back up and headed into the maze. However, unspoken horrors await him within…

Back at the mansion, Eliza blacked out a little after getting her blood drawn. However, she woke up from Rose splashing cold liquid over her face. Not knowing until she was fully awake, the cold liquid Rose splashed on her was blood.

"AHHHHHH!!!!!" Eliza screamed in fear.

"Shut up little bitch!" Rose yelled as she slapped her across the face.

"For fuck sakes! It's just blood! It's not like you were drowning in it! Now…After testing your blood. You are defiantly a virgin and worthy of going to the next stage of the test.

"H-How did you find out I'm a virgin by testing my blood?" Eliza asked hesitantly.

"None of your fucking business how I know. Just shut up and be ready for the next part of the test because this part no one has been able to pass." Rose said.

"Wh-What do you mean?" Eliza asked but was met with silence until Rose walked up behind Eliza and grabbed her chair.

Eliza was then dragged with the chair down stairs and then Rose tilted her chair upwards to see the dead women hanging from the chains with black eyes. In horror, Eliza shook uncontrollably at what she was seeing because some of these young women looked like her friends and neighbors but what shocked her the most was seeing her own mother's body up with them…

"Take a good long look…This is what happens when you can't pass this part of the test. These women and girls were tested without being virgins and failed in being Lord Key's Lock! The demonic energies that flowed through their veins consumed their souls and turned them into corpses. Lord Key demanded they be strung up like this for two reasons. One being his personal hobby in collecting these washed up dead whores. Two and this is for a more practical reason…as a warning to any volunteers trying to become Lord Key's Lock." Rose explained.

"So…If I don't pass…I'll be like them?" Eliza asked now starting to understand what's going to happen.

"Yes…Now, let's go to the basement to start second part of the test." Rose said as she began to drag the chair again.

"P-PLEASE!! I DON'T WANT TO DO THIS! PLEASE!! LET ME GO!!!!" Eliza begged as frightened tears poured out as she was pulled into the dark staircase leading down to the basement and then the door behind slammed shut…

Back at the maze, Mathew tried his best to navigate through the large labyrinth but each time he went further in he would have to turn around to find another route because he reached a dead end…

"Ugh! This is frustrating! If only I had a map of this thing. I could of gotten out by now." Mathew said as he continued searching for a way out.

Suddenly, Mathew heard the little girl's laughter again and looked around in a panic not knowing what was going to happen next. All of the sudden, dark hands busted out of the maze walls and tried to grab Mathew. Disturbed Mathew quickly dodged them and ran towards another direction. However, in his attempts to avoid being touched, the hands grabbed Mathew's knife, hatchet, and rope he had. Unable to get them back, Mathew continued running for his life…

"Hehehehe…You can run but you cannot survive." The girl's voice called as Mathew ran with all the strength he had.

Suddenly, Mathew fell through a trap door and into a hidden room. Groaning in pain, Mathew sat up and saw his surroundings. A light then turned on and Mathew saw an old man with an eye patch in front of him with a combat shotgun pointed at Mathew's face…

"Boy. You just couldn't resist, could ya?" The man said as he spat tobacco into a near trash can.

"W-Who are you? What's going on?" Mathew panicked.

"First thing I need you to do is put these on and sit in that chair over there. Once you do, I'll explain some shit." The man said as he tossed some handcuffs on Mathew's lap and with no choice Mathew did as the man demanded.

Mathew cuffed the handcuffs behind his back and got up slowly and walked over to the chair. Once he said down, the old man did the same with another chair nearby.

"First off. You tell me your name and then tell me why you are here. Once you do I'll answer your questions." The man said.

"M-My name is Mathew Sir…I'm from East City. I'm with the city's police department and came here with two of my colleagues upon request but both are dead and I have to find my missing girlfriend. So I came here to find a firearm to defend myself against the cult outside while I search for my girlfriend, Sarah." Mathew explained.

"Hmm…The first part I believe. However boy… That hogwash bullshit you said about your little girlfriend is nonsense." The man said while spitting again.

"IT'S NOT!!!" Mathew yelled.

"Mind your tone boy! Its bullshit and here's why! Anyone in this damn town is either a part of the cult or is dead by now. You can't sit there and say that your little girlfriend is still alive after everything you've been through. She's dead so get used to it and move on!" The man said which made Mathew stand up aggressively even with the old man still pointing his gun at Mathew.

"I'm going to find her even if she is dead! I've been through too much shit to even consider giving up now! I will find her and I will take her out of this fucking town!" Mathew shouted.

Suddenly, the man got up and put his shotgun on a nearby table and walked over to Mathew…

"Turn around." The man said as he pulled out a bowie knife from his sheath.

Mathew feared the man was going to kill him until he heard a clicking noise and the handcuffs fell off. Mathew then turned around and saw the man handing him a handgun with a magazine.

"You got what you came here for and I have no reason to kill you since you are not a part of the cult. However, I'm telling you this for your own good son…If you find a way out, leave. This place is going to become hell on earth. The cult, is nothing compare to what's going to happen once their demon king is resurrected." The man said.

"So you believe what they are saying is true?" Mathew asked.

"I don't just believe. I know…" The man said.

"What do you mean?" Mathew asked seeing the man walk back over to the chair to sit again.

"My name is Nate Howard. A former sergeant of the United States Army during the Vietnam War. I was dishonorably discharged for friendly fire against my commanding officer. Him and I found a hidden tomb in the jungle that held an artifact that looked like a big stone key…But when my commanding officer grab this key, his body changed…" Nate said.

"Changed? How?" Mathew asked.

"His teeth and skin changed shape, his eyes glowed yellow, and worst of all he killed the other soldiers with us. I ran out of the tomb with my gun in hand. Once he came out I shot at him but was unable to kill him. Other officers and soldiers came to our location once they heard my gun shots. However, he changed back to look normal and demanded the other soldiers take me into custody for friendly fire." Nate said as he continued his story.

"So what happened after that?" Mathew asked.

"The military court said since my unit has been fighting for long periods of time, my mind played tricks on me thinking I was firing at the enemy. However, even with them saying it was just a stress disorder, I knew the truth and protested but that got me nowhere. Once I saw that man again grinning in the courtroom, I lost my shit. I tried to kill him again with a military police's handgun but was stopped before I could us it. I was sentenced to twenty years for attempted murder and dishonorably discharged once I got out of prison." Nate said as his face expressed a look which made Mathew feel bad about what happened.

"I'm sorry Nate..." Mathew said.

"Sigh...Afterwards, I came back to my home town, Ghost, to live the rest of my days trying to forget about that...demon. However, last year I was getting groceries at the store and then...I saw him. He gave himself a new name, calling himself Key. I walked out of the store to confront him as he was in the middle of the street calling out to the people about the return of a demon king. He had followers around him and the police tried to arrest him but there was a woman with him and she had dark magical powers that killed the police. I couldn't believe my eyes but once Key saw me, he commanded the woman to come after me." Nate said as he continued his story.

"How'd you get away?" Mathew asked.

"By running to my father's old house which was left to me in his will but once I got here, the witch was yelling some sort of gibberish outside. Panicked, I grabbed my shotgun and was about to kill the bitch but something extremely weird happened. My house came to life and tried to kill me. Thinking back, that witch must have put a curse spell on the house." Nate said.

"The house tried to kill me too but I got to ask…Do you know anything about a little girl?" Mathew asked.

"…That's…my little sister or what used to be her." Nate said.

"Your little sister?" Mathew asked.

"Yes. She died when I was a teenager in this house. My father was at work and I was hanging out with my friends when it happened." Nate said.

"What…happened?" Mathew hesitated to ask because he was sure Nate wasn't too comfortable explaining.

"She was killed along with my mother by an intruder looking for valuables. My father was furious at me for not being there to protect them and sent me to a military school weeks later. What that witch did to this house must also be affecting my sister's spirit that hadn't moved on since. For months I venture out of this underground bunker to gather supplies to live but this house had limited food and water so I only have enough to last a few more weeks at best." Nate said.

"Have you tried to talk with your sister? Maybe we could move her soul from this place and she'll be at peace." Mathew suggested.

"Don't you think I already tired that!? She isn't the sister I used to know and it's all the fucking witch bitch's fault! Now that thing that looks like my little sister has complete control of the house and will kill anyone who walks inside because there is no way out with it changing the house constantly!" Nate shouted.

"There has to be a way to stop her. If we can get rid of this evil spirit then the house might go back to normal." Mathew said which got Nate thinking.

"…There might be a way but I'm going need your help." Nate said as he got up ready to end this once and for all…

Chapter 8

Nate and Mathew loaded up with what little they had. Mathew had the handgun that was given to him and Nate had his shotgun along with something he put in his pocket. Their plan was to exit out of the bunker's only way out which was a tunnel that made its way up to the kitchen.

"Look Mathew. Once we get through this tunnel and into the kitchen, I need you to distract that thing that looks like my little sister. While you're doing that, I'll find out where my sister's room is and find out what her spirit is attached to." Nate said.

"If the house is changing like you said, how will you find her room?" Mathew asked.

"It won't be easy but I'll find it. Once I find this thing, I'll burn it and it should get rid of the spirit." Nate said.

"You make it sound easy. Do you think burning whatever this thing might be will end the spirt and make the house go back to normal?" Mathew asked.

"Not really sure…but it's the best thing I can come up with. I don't know much about the paranormal but I assume ghosts, spirits, or demons are things that attach themselves to something to stay on this plane, right?" Nate asked

"I'm not sure myself…but I hope you are right. If this thing is attached to something in the house, we need to destroy it. I got to ask though…How the hell am I supposed to distract it?" Mathew asked.

"Try to make her chase you but because of the witch's spell on the house she won't be chasing you just for fun…" Nate said.

"I know. She'll try to kill me too." Mathew said.

"Try and keep her down stairs until I find her room upstairs. Hopefully something there will help put this spirit to rest and release us from this place." Nate said.

"Yeah..." Mathew agreed.

"Well...No use waiting. Ready?" Nate asked.

"Not really but we got no choice." Mathew said and Nate nodded as he opened the hatch that supposedly went to the kitchen.

Mathew went first so he can distract the demonic spirit so Nate could rush upstairs to find whatever the spirit was attached to. However, once Mathew reached the end of the tunnel, he didn't end up in the kitchen like originally planned. Mathew found himself in the attic and didn't know how...

"Nate I think the house changed and-" Mathew said as he turned around but he noticed that not only Nate was nowhere to be seen but also the tunnel he went through was gone as well.

Suddenly, the room got very cold and Mathew could feel the evil atmosphere around him.

Grabbing his gun, Mathew prepared himself for a confrontation with the demon spirit. Then suddenly, Mathew heard the laughter…

"Hehehe. Stupid little man. I know about your little plan but don't worry, nothing in that little girl's room is keeping me here. In fact the only thing keeping this spirit here is this little girl's older brother." The demon spirit said in Mathew's head.

"Just let her go! She needs to move on!" Mathew yelled.

"Do you actually believe in the crap you are saying? Or are you just looking for a way out just like the others that dared to enter this place?" The demon spirit questioned.

"Look! Nate's sister has suffered enough! I know about the witch that summoned you! Please let Nate's sister go so we can leave! This has to stop and the cult's plan with the demon king needs to-"

Mathew said until the spirit suddenly appeared in front of Mathew and slammed his body against the wall pinning him there.

Mathew coughed up blood on impact with the wall but he looked at the demon spirit even in his pain. In front of him was the little girl but her face was cut up, her eyes were black, and all around her was dark smoke pouring out of her skin. Her hand gripped Mathew's throat as long black nails dug into his flesh making Mathew bleed a little.

"You want out to stop the revival of the demon king and save your little girly-friend. I overheard you and the little girl's brother talking. You have no chance of stopping the return of the demon king, let alone leaving this place that I control!" The demon spirit said while firmly holding Mathew's neck against the wall.

"W-Why d-didn't y-y-you tr-try to k-kill us t-then?" Mathew struggled to stay as he was being strangled.

"Because! This little brat's spirit that I've been attached to from the curse has been keeping me from killing that old man! Now she's been resisting me to kill you! It's infuriating!!!!" The demon spirit shouted as she slammed Mathew again against the wall making it crack but also putting Mathew in severe pain.

Meanwhile, Nate wound up in the kitchen from the hole behind a counter but didn't see Mathew anywhere. He assumed Mathew was already trying to distract the demon spirit in the house so he wasted no time going to his sister's old room. Once he made it there, the door was locked but instead of being subtle, Nate shot the door knob with his shotgun and kicked the door in.

"Alright, Mary. Please give me a sign to help you." Nate said as he began to look around.

The last time Nate had been in his sister's room was years ago but everything was left the same way since the day she died. Regardless, Nate had no time to remember the past since he's trusting Mathew to hold off the demon that's controlling his sister's spirit. So Nate began his search…

Mathew was trying his best to stall the evil spirit but it was a fruitless battle as the demon flung Mathew around the attic like a ragdoll. The demon spirit's eyes burned with fury as she slammed Mathew's body to the ground. Mathew was in pain but soon was afraid as the boxes around him had snakes pouring out of them and they were breathing some sort of dark smoke.

"Now you die!" The demon spirit said with venom in her voice.

Multiple snakes bit Mathew on the arms, legs, and neck but Mathew quickly yanked them off as he stood up and pointed the handgun at the demon spirit in front of him.

"Hahahahaha! Are you that stupid? You can't shoot spirits pathetic human!" The demon spirit said.

"No but I can try to make it harder for you as you made it for me." Mathew said as he fired three rounds into the wall of the attic and outside light came shining in.

"NO!!" The demon spirit shouted as the floors came to life and grabbed Mathew with shadowy hands. His body was forced down and one shadow hand the demon spirit controlled grabbed Mathew's gun and flung it away.

"Now. Let's see what you truly fear!" The demon spirit said with a sadistic tone as one of the dark hands that was holding Mathew ripped off a chunk of flesh from his arm.

"AHHHHHHHHH!!!!!!!!" Mathew screamed as blood poured out.

"HAHAHAHAHAHA! How sweet. I want MORE!!" The demon spirit shouted as more hands began to rip more flesh little by little.

"FUCK!! AHHHHH!! STOPPP PLEASE!!" Mathew begged.

Meanwhile, Nate searched the whole room but couldn't think of anything the spirit might be attached to until he came across his sister's old diary. It looked like it was used recently because there was fresh ink written on the last page of the diary.

"Nate…If you are reading this, you know I'm not alive. You are the only one that can send me to be with Mommy and Daddy. I feel so cold here but as long as you are with me, I'm not alone. I miss Mommy and Daddy though. Please help me see them again…Please take me to them." The dairy said as Nate read it.

"Take you…to them? What does that mean?" Nate said but then heard the screams of Mathew and ran to his aid.

From the sounds of the screams, Nate assumed Mathew was in the attic and rushed to help. However, once Nate got to the attic he saw the demon spirit that looked like his sister, Mary, with a hand on Mathew's head.

"Get away from him!" Nate shouted.

"Aw! Hello Brother." The demon spirit greeted.

"I'm not your brother you demon! What have you done to Mathew!?" Nate demanded.

"I put him under a deep hallucination to where he thinks he's being torn apart but that's the fun part. Once he wakes up, he will experience true fear after I make him kill you!" The demon spirit said in a twisted sounding voice.

"How are you going to do that?!" Nate demanded.

"By offering to stop his pain once he snaps and kills you but after he does I'm going to make his fucking head explode with images of hell!" The demon spirit said with a sadistic grin.

"It sickens me to see something as foul as you taking control of my little sister's spirit. You are just as horrifying as the demon calling himself Key." Nate said with his shotgun pointed at the demon spirit.

"Hahahahahaha! You don't understand what Key is. I've been summoned from the deepest parts of Hell and even I know about what's going to happen when Key find's his Lock.

"I know…The demon king's revival and Armageddon along with it." Nate said but suddenly his shotgun was knocked out of his hands and was pushed against the wall by an invisible but strong force.

"YOU KNOW NOTHING! The demon king's revival is more than a simple apocalypse! It's the birth of a new Hell. Where blood, fire, and darkness will reign. All will fear the pain as demons like me will pour forth and enslave any mankind that survives." The demon spirit said as black blood poured from her mouth.

"You...will...not..." Nate struggled to say.

"Will not what big brother? Come on say what you need to say before I send Mathew to tear your head off." The demon spirit said.

"SUCEED!!" Nate shouted as he pulled something out his pocket and it was revealed to be a flashbang grenade.

As it hit the floor, the flashbang grenade blinded the demon spirit and woke up Mathew. The demon noticed and released its grip on Nate by mistake. Nate took advantage of the lapse of the demon spirit's control and rushed over to Mathew. In a split second, Nate pushed Mathew through the wall of the attic where it was shot earlier with all his strength.

Mathew and Nate fell through the wall and outside while the spirit tried to recapture the two by piercing Nate's back with a demonic hand. However, Nate turned and grabbed the manifested spirit's body in a hug, dragging her into the light outside.

"NOOOOOO!!!!!!!!" The demon spirit shouted as Nate fell to the ground along with Mathew before him.

The demon spirit died when the light hit it and Nate's sister's spirit was now free from the demon's hold of her. When Nate and Mathew landed on the property grounds…only one lived from the fall.

"Mmm…What happened?" Mathew said as he sat up in pain from the impact of the ground.

However, Mathew saw Nate's lifeless body on the ground but what really surprised Mathew the most was seeing not just Nate's sister's spirit but Nate's spirit as well. He was holding Mary's hand and both seemed happy as they took their leave into the sky. In this touching moment, Mathew was glad the nightmare was over. He was a little sad that Nate had died but was happy that his spirit and Mary's were now together again.

After Mathew got up, he planned on going back into the house to retrieve the firearms left behind. However, the house erupted in black flames and terrifying roar could be heard inside.

"YOU WILL DIE!!! ALL HAIL THE DEMON KING!" The house said as it burned down to the ground.

Mathew assumed the demonic spirit died after the house burned down but knew the guns inside are probably useless now. With no other options he decided to leave. He knew he had to find his girlfriend but after everything he had just seen, he was now a full believer in the paranormal.

"If this demonic spirit was real, then maybe the cult are really trying to resurrect the demon king. I thought it was all bullshit but now I know…I have to find a way of stopping them. Otherwise, it won't matter if I find Sarah. I can't let that demon, Key, revive the demon king." Mathew thought as he left determined to stop Key now…No matter the cost.

Meanwhile, back at the mansion where Eliza was being held, she was being tortured by Rose. The second part of Eliza's test was to see if normal means torture would awaken the demon Lock within her. However, hours had past and throughout all the screams, tears, and blood, Rose was starting to get impatient…

"DAMN IT!" Rose shouted as she flung a metal tray that had a variety of tools on it against a nearby wall of the basement.

"Pant…Pant…Pant…" Eliza breathed heavily as blood dripped from her face slowly.

"We don't have much time! You need to awaken Lock! If you don't, Key will have to search again and we won't be able to revive the demon king in time!" Rose shouted as she shook Eliza.

"I…I'm n-not Lock." Eliza said with defiance in her eyes.

"Stubborn girl. I'll be back with another tool that I'm sure will work. Don't you dare try to fucking escape or you will be begging me for death!" Rose shouted as she took her leave and closed the door behind her.

"I got to get out of here." Eliza said as she wiggled and struggled in her chair that she was strapped in.

Suddenly, a weak leg on the chair broke and Eliza fell with the chair. Luckily, her hand broke free and used it to get the straps off her other arm and legs. Once she got up, she looked around. There was a bloodied knife Rose used on her earlier to carve satanic runes in her flesh to help the awakening of Lock but was on the ground along with other tools when Rose flung them.

"This should help…" Eliza said as she picked up the bloody blade in a shivering mess from all the pain she had to endure.

"I got to get out of here. Hopefully, that Rose woman won't find me. I know my family has a few cars inside our garage. So if I can just get there, maybe I can start it up with the car keys that are hanging on the wall." Eliza thought as she cautiously opened the door and peered out.

"Make sure she stays in the room. If you do anything to her while I prepare my next tool, you will be sorry!" Rose said to a cult member outside the room.

"Yes ma'am." The cult member said and then Rose took her leave.

"Please! I'll do what I fucking want. The mayor's daughter? Who can say they got with someone like that? Hahaha." The cult member said as he walked towards the room Eliza was in.

Eliza was scared about the man that was coming in to have his way with her but she quickly hid on the other side of the door so the man couldn't find her once he entered…

"Hey little girl. Daddy's here." The cult man said but then saw she wasn't in her chair and panicked.

However, once the man turned, Eliza stabbed his groin with all the strength she had. The man had fallen to the ground in pain as blood fiercely poured out. Eliza wasted no time as she ran out of the room and locked the door behind her. However, she no longer had the knife because she left it in the cult member when she stabbed him.

"Okay…I just got to get upstairs and head towards the garage." Eliza said as she made her way towards the staircase which lead to the first floor of the house.

"All I'm saying is we need to distinguish ourselves to Key if we are going to be in his inner circle." A cult member said outside the door.

"I know but how? I mean come on! The two loyalists he had with him offered a lot of sacrifices and one of them has magic powers. I don't think we could compete with that." The other cult member said.

"Maybe your right. Come on, let's go out for a smoke." The first cult member said and the two left their post making Eliza's escape easier.

However, they went out the front door and were probably still there so Eliza couldn't go out that way. So she stuck with her original plan and went towards the garage to find a vehicle and drive away from her home town before she was killed.

Suddenly, she heard a door slamming and realized it was Rose coming out of a room on the second floor of the mansion. Eliza quickly entered the kitchen to avoid being seen. However, once inside of the kitchen she saw something horrifying. A body was on the kitchen counter cut open and from the looks of it, his heart was removed.

"Oh my God!" Eliza said in a low tone while covering her mouth at the sight of the mutilated body in front of her.

Suddenly, Eliza saw something in front of the body. There was a piece of paper that had instructions about removing a heart. It didn't take Eliza long to realize this was a cadaver for when the cult would have to remove her heart. She guessed the cult needed her heart intact if she was Lock but she was not going to let them take it out even if she was.

Suddenly, Eliza heard the kitchen door knob behind her start to turn and she quickly hid behind the counter. Still covering her mouth, she was trying to keep quiet as footsteps walked in. Sweat poured down her face as she couldn't help but breathe heavily.

"Eliza?...I know you left your room…Come out and I promise not to rip out one of your eyes." Rose said while looking around the kitchen.

However, once Eliza heard Rose walking towards her, she quickly moved to the other side of the counter before Rose could find her. She could feel Rose's eyes searching and the atmosphere was thick with malice as Rose knocked over pots and pans in a rage.

"Once I find you, I'm going to cut off your fucking feet so you won't get away again! Do you hear me!?" Rose shouted as she took her leave to search for Eliza in another room.

Relieved she avoided detection, Eliza got back up and went through the back door of the kitchen which lead to the dining room. However, once she entered the room, the whole house went dark. Rose had turned off the power to frighten Eliza into a panic and reveal herself to the cult that was now searching for her.

"We got to find the bitch. You, search the dining room while check upstairs." A cult member said behind a door to another cult member and Eliza quickly crawled underneath the dining room table with the long tablecloth.

The sun was near setting and made the whole room bright enough for shadows to be seen from under the table through the tablecloth. The legs of the cult member was walking around the table and Eliza saw fearfully because he was also carrying a machete.

Tears were forming in Eliza's eyes because she was afraid of what this man might do to her. If he was like the other man from down in the basement, he would try to have his way with her too.

However, she began to crawl the other direction as the man began to walk down the other way.

Suddenly, the tablecloth was revealed and the cult member saw Eliza and a sadistic grin came on his face as panic came on Eliza's. The man jumped on the table and Eliza crawled for her life as the man ran down the long table laughing. Suddenly, Eliza's pants got caught on a chair which made her fall to the ground. The cult member was now above her once he saw the chair where she was had moved.

"Hahahahahaha! I found the little bitch! Time to die!" The man shouted as he thrusted his machete through the table and towards Eliza.

However, the blade didn't reach her but barely as the tip of the machete was near her eye. The blade pulled out of the table and the cult member kneeled down on the table to look through the hole he made.

"Hello little bitch. I hope you are ready. I'm going to cut you up and make you die slowly. Hahahaha!" The cult member said until…

"AHHHHHHHHHH!!!!!!!" The cult member screamed as his body boiled and smoked.

"What did I fucking tell you!? Don't kill the girl!" Rose said from the other side of the table.

The body of cult member fell on top of the hole he made and blood dripped down onto Eliza's horrified face. Suddenly, the whole table was flipped with Rose's magic and crashed on the other side of the dining room.

"Good. I found you before these fucking untrained animals got to you." Rose said with a sadistic smile as she was about to grab Eliza but she got up and ran away.

"I DON'T THINK SO!" Rose shouted as she tried recapturing Eliza by conjuring dark magical chains at Eliza but she avoided them. However, one chain came close as it grabbed her shirt but it ripped and Eliza still managed to get away.

"Stay away!" Eliza yelled as her eyes glowed bright blue and an invisible force hit Rose.

Rose was sent flying into the wall which made her head hit making her go unconscious. Eliza grabbed her head in pain at what just happened. She had no idea how she did that but realized something was wrong as her eyes and nose was bleeding a little. Whatever the case maybe…she knew this was her chance to escape.

Chapter 9

Mathew's choice to go into the haunted house was a fruitless one because he wasn't able to get any firearms. Regardless, he did get some information about Key and how he was turned into a demon. However, this still complicated things.

On one hand Mathew knows he needs to stop Key and his cult or they will bring the demon king to life. However, on the other hand he doesn't know how he's going to stop them. At first, Mathew thought the cult's mission about the demon king was just nonsense and an excuse to kill off innocent people but after seeing that demonic spirit in Nate's house, Mathew was now a full believer.

"I don't know how…but I got to stop them. I need to find Sarah but that won't matter if the cult succeeds in their plan. Let's see…If I remember right, someone named Lock would be needed for

their plan to work. So all I got to do is stop them from finding this Lock person and all will be good. The question is how? Regardless, I need to go back to the neighborhoods and find myself a weapon of some sort because I literally have nothing." Mathew thought as he made his way back towards the neighborhood where he first started…

After being attacked by Eliza's hidden power, Rose finally woke up from being hit. In pain, Rose was furious at Eliza but realized she had to be Lock now after discovering the power that had awakened within Eliza. Rose then tried to use her magic to heal herself but something was wrong…

"What the fuck! Why isn't my magic working!?...This must be that little bitch's fault! I got to find her…" Rose said until her radio started saying something and she turned it up to listen to what it was saying.

"To the cult of the demon king…The time is near so in order for our plan of the demon king's revival to happen I need more sacrifices. So kill all in your path and I will reward the ones that survive a place within the new hell amongst the inner council with the demon king." Key announced then all of the sudden the radio played static and Rose knew the tower must have been knocked out.

"Damn it! If I don't hurry and deliver Lock to Lord Key then the plan will be ruined if the cult kills her beforehand." Rose said as she angrily went after Eliza again and she had a pretty good idea where she might be...

The sun was setting and Eliza finally got away from Rose in her attempt to escape. Eliza found the garage but was disheartened when she saw the vehicles were missing except one. However, the vehicle that was there in the garage was a police car but it was stripped of its wheels, doors, and strobe lights. It only had its police design and that's was what made Eliza recognize it as a police car...

"Damn it...What should I do now?" Eliza said in frustration but then saw something on the ground near the car.

"What's this?" Eliza said as she picked up a file of some sorts.

In the file, it had pictures of police officers and info about them including their names and ranks. Two of the three photos had red x marks on the faces and Eliza looked at the one that didn't have an x mark on it...

"Officer Mathew..." Eliza said while looking at the photo. Something told her he was still alive and might be able to help her if she was able to get out.

However, that was easier said than done because the garage door was locked up and Eliza couldn't get out that way. She tried the electronic button that opened the door but no dice. She then got a crowbar nearby and wedged it in the bottom of the door to try and lift it. Suddenly, the door behind her opened and Rose came through breathing in pain…and anger.

"You bitch! I should be happy now that I found out that you are Lock but your attack fucking hurt!" Rose shouted as she threw a nearby tool at Eliza but she dodged it.

"I-I'm sorry! Please don't kill me!" Eliza begged as she ran towards a corner.

"What made matters worse is that your inner demonic power nullified my magic! After all the training I've done over the years with Lord Key's guidance…All of it was fucking thrown away!" Rose shouted as she picked up a large pipe wrench from the work bench.

"P-Please! I'll do anything you ask just don't-" Eliza pleaded but was startled by Rose slamming the wrench into the dismantled car between the two.

"SHUT THE FUCK UP! The only way I can redeem myself now to Lord Key is taking your sorry ass to him! However, that's going to be a problem now because of his radio announcement!" Rose shouted.

"R-Radio announcement?" Eliza asked.

"Lord Key doesn't know yet you are Lock and because of time running out, he's ordered the cult to kill each other in favor of finding you! The cult is happy to do this because they want to be in Lord Key's inner circle! However, I can't reach him on the radio now because those fucking idiots outside knocked out the radio tower!" Rose explained.

"S-So what n-now?" Eliza nervously asked.

"Now we have to find our way to the damn cemetery! That's where Lord Key is having the ritual to summon the demon king! However, the demon king hasn't given him your location so Lord Key demanded more sacrifices to appease the demon king but the cult is taking it the wrong way and creating fucking chaos outside!" Rose said.

"So what you are saying is that because the cult is causing havoc we can't leave?" Eliza boldly asked.

"What I'm saying is that we are in a fucking shit storm! And since I don't have my magic to escort you to Lord Key, we have to do this the old fashion way!" Rose said as she pointed to the door.

"Wait! What?! You expect me to go outside and possibly get killed by your band of lunatics and-" Eliza panicked until Rose thrown the wrench she had towards her direction and smashed a counter next to Eliza

"That's exactly what I'm fucking saying! Lord Key needs you to revive the demon king! Even if it kills me, you will go to him intact or our plans won't come to fruition!" Rose shouted.

"I'm not going with you! If all you care about is reviving the demon king, then I would rather die just so your fucking plan fails!" Eliza shouted back gaining her bravery against Rose.

"ENOUGH! It's time to stop with the damn games! You will do as I say or you'll regret it!" Rose shouted as the two stared at each other intensely.

The air in the garage was thick with conflict as Rose and Eliza waited in anticipation for the other's move. Eliza's eyes glowed again but unlike before, she wasn't able to use her power as she coughed up blood. Rose took advantage of this distraction and rushed over to Eliza.

"GET AWAY!!" Eliza shouted as her hair was being grabbed by Rose.

"AHHHHH!!!!!!" Rose screamed as she tried to subdue Eliza but she was resisting.

Eliza clawed at Rose's face in defense but Rose retaliated by slamming Eliza's head a few times into the garage wall violently. Eliza was bleeding from her forehead but managed to grab hold of Rose's eye and rip it out. In anguishing pain, Rose let go of Eliza and grabbed her face.

"FUCKKKKKKKK!!!!!!!!!! DAMN YOU BITCH!!" Rose shouted as Eliza escaped the garage. However, Rose was in pursuit of Eliza regardless of her pain as blood dripped down her face.

"Hahahaha! Fucking bitch! That hurt! But don't worry, I'm not going to kill you…I'm going to make you suffer before we leave!" Rose called out with a sadistic twisted smile because malice was all she was thinking about now as she made her way back into the house…

Meanwhile, Mathew finally got back to the neighborhood but was shocked to see what happened. Houses were being burned down as cultists were killing each other in anarchy. Mathew had no idea what was going on until he found a near death cultist behind a house and went to him for answers…

"What's going on!?" Mathew questioned.

"L-Lord Key s-s-said…F-For mo-more s-sacrifices…" The cultist said as he gave his final breath and died right in front of Mathew.

"This…is beyond madness…" Mathew said to himself until someone came rushing on him with a knife to try to kill him.

The cultist tackled Mathew and tried forcing the knife into Mathew chest. However, Mathew resisted and managed to out muscle the cultist. The cultist got pushed off and Mathew hit his face with all the strength he had. It wasn't enough to knock the cultist out but Mathew managed to knock the knife out of the cultist's hand.

"RAAAA!!" The cultist screamed as he got his balance back from being hit but was too late because Mathew grabbed the knife and slit the cultist's throat.

Bleeding rapidly, the cultist died and fell to the ground. Mathew was breathing heavily from defending himself. Suddenly, Mathew heard gun shots and people in the streets were being shot at and rushed inside a house before he got shot. Looking outside from within the house, Mathew couldn't believe the cult was killing itself just because of Key ordering it…or perhaps this was a part of Key's plan all along.

"I can't believe this is happening…" Mathew said as he looked out the window.

"I know, right?" Someone said behind Mathew which made him turn defensively.

"Chill bro. I'm just in here until the heat outside dies down." The man said.

"Aren't you with the cult?" Mathew asked.

"Yeah…I was." The man said.

"What do you mean?" Mathew asked.

"After Key gave the order to kill ourselves for the demon king, I knew right there and then that we were being played. However, those guys outside…followed the command like damn dogs. I wanted out so I hid in this house until the killing died down and I could slip away." The man said.

"Where are you going to go?" Mathew asked.

"To find the real person that needs to be killed…Key." The man said.

"Aren't you afraid I might tell the rest of the cult?" Mathew asked to keep his identity secret.

"Not really since you are that cop that came yesterday morning." The man said.

"H-How did you know?" Mathew asked.

"Dude. Isn't obvious? You don't look like any of the locals with that haircut of yours plus I saw you coming into town that day." The man said.

"So…What now?" Mathew asked.

"You want to stop Key? I do too. Let me come with you." The man said.

"…" Mathew hesitated.

"I understand you don't trust me but believe me when I say I want out of this failing cult and I want the leader dead for treating us like his play things." The man said.

"Fine…What's your name?" Mathew asked.

"Daniel." Daniel said.

"Mathew." Mathew responded back as the two shook hands.

"So are you armed?" Daniel asked.

"Just this knife I got off the cultist that attacked me earlier." Mathew said.

"I have a handgun but no ammo." Daniel said.

"Then we need to arm up before we try to find Key. Any ideas where he might be?" Mathew asked.

"I was told before the order to kill ourselves to stay away from the local cemetery so we should head over there once the killing outside dies down and-" Daniel said until a body came crashing through the window from outside.

"RAHHH!" The cult member screamed as he got up bloodied with a bat in hand.

The cult member tried to attack Daniel but was stopped when Mathew stabbed the cult member's chest from behind. The cult member died and Mathew pulled out the knife.

"We need to leave." Mathew said.

"Y-Yeah." Daniel agreed as he was startled on how easy it was for Mathew to kill someone but didn't think too much into it as he followed Mathew out the back door.

The two made their way towards the direction of the cemetery. However, it was on the other side of town and untold obstacles awaited them along the way. Neither truly trusted each other. Mathew believed even though Daniel was now a former cult member, he could still turn on Mathew if he wanted to. Daniel though, felt Mathew would kill him once they found Key or even before then. However, even though they were cautious of the other, both had the same goal in mind...to stop Key's plan.

Meanwhile back at the mansion Eliza was still being pursued by Rose yet again but this time was different because Rose isn't able to use her magic. Also, due to Eliza resisting earlier, Rose lost an eye. However, even with no magic and being half blind, Rose was hell bent on finding Eliza and take her to Key at the cemetery. However, Rose wanted compensation for losing her magic and eye with Eliza's suffering...

"ELIZA!!!!!! WHERE THE FUCK ARE YOU!?" Rose screamed in furious rage as she searched the mansion's first floor.

Eliza was on the second floor though. She felt like she needed to hide until she found an opening to escape the building but that was easier said than done. Rose was stalking the first floor and if she tried to make her escape then Eliza might be caught by Rose.

Rose then busted through the kitchen in anger. She grabbed the nearby first aid kit and tended to her face that was injured. After she was done, Rose saw on a nearby kitchen counter a knife and a sickening smile crept on Rose's face.

"Hahaha. I'm going to enjoy stabbing this in your limbs over and over again! That way you won't fucking move and I'll drag you by the hair to Lord Key." Rose said in a sadistic tone as she made her way out the kitchen.

After searching everywhere Rose assumed Eliza wasn't on the first floor and made her way up the stairs. Unfortunately, Eliza chose to hide in a closet in front of the stair case. Her eyes watched as Rose slowly made her way up. Blood was dripping down Rose's face as foul giggling could be heard from her. Eliza's heart raced as she witnessed Rose finally reaching the top of the stairs and in front of the closet.

Sweat poured out of every part of Eliza's body as fear was engulfing her entire body. Suddenly, Eliza heard a man shouting from down stairs and assumed it was a cult member…

"For the demon king! HAHAHAHAHA!" The cult member shouted as he ran up the stairs to try and kill Rose but she was ready for him as she used the kitchen knife to stab the man's chest and rend it up through his body in a quick motion. Blood sprayed towards Rose and some blood managed to make its way through the closet door to Eliza's face.

"Well…Looks like they know my location. I better find this little bitch before the cult does." Rose said as she walked away down a hall.

Eliza dared to venture out once she felt the coast was clear. The body in front of her though was mutilated from Rose's knife. If it wasn't for Eliza seeing dead bodies before, this would have bothered her more than it was now. However, now was not the time to dwell on these thoughts. Eliza then descended down the staircase and towards the front door.

"I'm almost free." Eliza softly said to herself in relief as she crept up to the front door.

However, once Eliza turned the knob of the door and looked outside, what she saw killed what little hope of escape she had left…

"This…This can't be real…" Eliza said with tears rolling down her eyes as she witnessed not only dead bodies all over her front lawn and driveway but also seeing more cultists trying to kill each other from not too far away…

"You're not getting away from me this time bitch!" Rose shouted from within the mansion.

Eliza turned to see but before she had time to react a shot gun blast was shot near her head and blown off the side of the door frame next to Eliza. From behind was a cultist with a bloody face and was carrying a double barrel shot gun smiling uncontrollably while reloading.

"Get the fuck in here now!" Rose shouted and Eliza complied even though it wasn't willingly but Eliza still feared for her life as she dashed inside and towards the living room.

"DIE!!!!!" The cultist screamed as he went after Eliza but didn't see Rose quickly coming up and stabbing his neck.

"I don't have time for this." Rose said as she sliced out the cultist's neck and left him for dead on the ground.

Picking up the gun, Rose put her knife away in her pocket and walked towards the living room. However, as soon as Rose opened the door...

"AHHHHH!!!!" Eliza screamed as she slammed Rose with a lamp against her head.

"FUCK!" Rose yelled in pain as she tried to point the gun at Eliza but she quickly kicked it away from Rose's hands.

Rose quickly pulled out the knife again and sliced Eliza's arm before she ran away. In agony, Eliza quickly got away and even with blood running down her arm she needed to put some distance between her and Rose.

"I don't care what it's like outside! Anywhere is better than here!" Eliza thought as she rushed towards the front door again to escape again.

Suddenly, as soon as Eliza opened the door…Key was in front of her smiling. Terror from the likes Eliza never known before overwhelmed her entire body as Key simply touched her head and Eliza fell to the ground unconscious…

"L-Lord Key!" Rose said in shock.

"Rose…I've come to retrieve Lock. The demon king finally gave me the vision of her identity and it's this girl right here just as I suspected all along." Key said.

"Y-Yes my lord. She has power within her and was able to take away my magic. I have no doubt she is Lock as well my lord." Rose said as she dropped her gun and walked over to pick Eliza up.

"Now we must go. The ritual is about to start as soon as night comes." Key said.

Rose nodded in agreement as she followed him out of the mansion and towards a vehicle. As they drove off towards the cemetery, the sun had finally reached its end and night time was near…

Chapter 10

Mathew saw the daylight was fading as he traveled with Daniel in the direction of the cemetery. Even though the main objective was to stop Key before the lunar eclipse ended, both knew they needed more weaponry than what they had…

"So Mathew…I'm grateful you saved me back at the neighborhood but do you actually have a plan to stop Key?" Daniel asked.

"Well I figured since we don't have much to work with, we'd better stock up." Mathew explained.

"How? The cult has all the guns and ammunition in this town. It would be risky but I think we should go after members that have guns and ammo." Daniel said.

"That would be foolish. Even though I'm a trained officer, all I have is a knife and you have a handgun with no bullets. No, I got a safer way to get a little of what we need." Mathew said.

"What do you mean?" Daniel asked.

"Well…I couldn't believe I thought about this earlier but I think we should head to the sheriff's office. Even though he was a part of the cult, he might still have some ammo or firearms within the building." Mathew said.

"What about Key? If we don't hurry to stop him before the eclipse he might summon the demon king! All he needs is Lock and with all the killing going on, he might find out who Lock really is!" Daniel panicked.

"True but there are flaws in his plan." Mathew said.

"Which are?" Daniel asked.

"Assuming what Key said was true about finding Lock if the cult kills enough for him…The problem is Lock might be killed before or after he finds out. Not only that but even if he finds out whom Lock really is, Key would have to go through the mess he created with the cult just to get to him or her." Mathew said.

"It's a female." Daniel said.

"...How do you know about that?" Mathew asked getting a tad suspicious.

"Lord...I-I mean Key told us it would be female but that doesn't matter since...you know." Daniel said.

"Know what?" Mathew questioned now stopping and Daniel stopped walking too.

"She would have to be a virgin. Most tried to become Key's Lock but failed after their tests. I only heard rumors but ladies young and old tried to be Key's Lock and died afterwards. Even women from other cities and counties came too but failed also...but like I said, they're only rumors." Daniel said.

"So is there anyone that's still a virgin in this town?" Mathew asked.

"Not that I'm aware of but we should still keep moving. Time is wasting and we need to stop Key before it's too late." Daniel said as he walked ahead and Mathew followed but was getting more suspicious by the second.

"Is Daniel still on my side? Or is he still loyal to Key? I should keep a close eye on him just in case." Mathew thought as he continued to follow Daniel.

Suddenly, a loud explosion could be heard from a distance and Mathew along with Daniel turn towards its direction…

"What was that?" Daniel asked.

"Sounds like a pipe bomb. Awfully extreme for killing someone though." Mathew said.

Five minutes earlier, Rose and Key were driving down the highway leading towards the cemetery.

However, the cemetery was still a few miles away and with Eliza still knocked out in the back seat of the car, time was running out…

"Lord Key. The moon is out now and it's a full one just like you predicted." Rose said looking out the window.

"Yes…In the next two hours the eclipse will begin. After the moon is fully eclipsed we only have ten minutes to perform the ritual to summon the demon king once I take Lock's heart and enter the doorway." Key said.

"How far are we from the cemetery?" Rose asked.

"Not far. Just a few miles. We should be able to reach there in time before the-" Key said until the car ran over a homemade pipe bomb mine and crashed the car into a light pole on the side of the road.

"AHHHH!!!!!" Rose screamed as she crawled out of the car in agony because her leg was broken.

"Hahahahahaha! I got another one! Lord Key will be pleased once I kill you! HAHAHAHA!" A cult member psychotically laughed.

However, on the other side of the car there was a loud sound from the door being busted off and went flying. Key then emerged with Eliza in his arms. Key then laid Eliza down next to Rose and looked at the cult member with fury in his face.

"L-Lord Key!? I-I didn't know it was you! P-Please forgiv-" The cult member said until demonic nails extended out of Key's fingers and pierced the cult member's arm.

"AHHHHHHHHH!!!!!!!!" The cult member screamed but then screamed even more when Key ripped the arm completely off making blood spray out of the cult member.

"You dare delay the revival of the demon king?! I'll make you suffer!" Key said in a demonic tone as the cultist's blood then turned into flames and then made the body explode.

"I'm sorry about this my dear. Let me take care of you." Key said as he placed his hands on Rose and instantly healed her with his demonic magic.

Rose was amazed by Key's magic that not only healed her and mended her broken leg but also returning her eye she lost earlier. Key then healed the injuries on Eliza but for some reason took more time because she wasn't human.

"That took more out of me than I thought. Still, I should have enough power to open the doorway with Lock's heart." Key said.

"I'm grateful my lord. I promise to take better care to make sure your plan is fulfilled." Rose said.

"I'm sure you will my dear. However, I think you'll be better use to me if you find us a vehicle while we walk towards our destination." Key commanded as he picked up the unconscious Eliza and carried her over his shoulder.

"Yes my lord." Rose said as she followed him.

Meanwhile, Mathew and Daniel continued their journey to the sheriff's office back in town. However, once they reached the town's main street, they couldn't believe what happened.

"My god…" Mathew said in astoundment as buildings were on fire and a few cultists were looting what they could.

"Follow my lead and act the roll until we are away from the others." Daniel said as he pointed his handgun at Mathew's back and Mathew nodded as he agreed to be a pretend hostage.

As the two walked into the heart of the town, the other cultists saw the two walking in but they figured Daniel was still a cultist and was about to kill Mathew somewhere else. However, even though the other cultists were believing in Daniel and Mathew's act, it still made both of them cautious. If the cult caught wind it was all faked the both Mathew and Daniel would be killed. Suddenly, one cultist called out to both of them once they were almost away…

"Hey Danny boy! Isn't that the fucking cop?" A cultist asked as he walked towards them but Daniel and Mathew kept walking trying to act like they didn't hear him but in all actually they were ignoring him to get away.

"Hey I'm talking to you! Are you deaf!? Face me you piece of shit!" The cultist demanded as he unsheathed his large knife.

"Shit! He's catching on!" Mathew panicked in a low tone

"Just run as soon as I take the gun off of you." Daniel whispered back.

"IF YOU DON'T TURN AROUND NOW, I'M GOING TO KILL YOU AND THAT FUCKING COP!" The cultist shouted in anger.

"Now!" Daniel said and Mathew ran for it.

Daniel then turned around and pointed his gun at the cultist.

"What the fuck!? What are you doing?!" The cultist demanded.

"Stay back or I'll shoot!" Daniel shouted.

"You damn idiot! You really joined up with that pig asshole?" The cultist said as the other two cultist joined him but kept their distance in case Daniel's gun was loaded.

"I told you stay back!" Daniel shouted.

Meanwhile, Mathew finally found the sheriff's office that was ransacked by cultists but was abandoned now. Mathew hurried inside to find something in order to help Daniel. Even though

Daniel was from the cult, he saved Mathew and he needed to help him before the cult kills Daniel.

Mathew then saw a large locker towards the back of the sheriff's office that was beat up from the cult's attempt to open it before but was still locked up with a padlock. Mathew took out his knife to try and jimmy it open but after a minute of trying the knife broke into pieces with a fraction of the tip still stuck in the keyhole.

"Fuck!" Mathew shouted because he accidently cut his hand with the broken knife once it slipped out of his hands.

Mathew then grabbed the padlock and used the small shard of the knife blade to pick the lock. After another two minutes of trying…

"Click." The lock sounded and opened up.

"Yes!" Mathew cheered as he opened up the locker.

Inside had a note that said not to use and had a large bag wrapped around something. After ripping open the bag, Mathew revealed an assault rifle with two clips next to it. Mathew quickly grabbed the assault rifle and put the two clips in his pocket.

Suddenly, Mathew heard running footsteps outside and realized it was Daniel running away from the cultists after they found out he was faking with his gunpoint against them.

Mathew rushed out and saw Daniel being chased. In one quick action, Mathew pointed the assault rifle at the cultist, loaded the first clip, and fired upon them. Without realizing it until it was too late, the cultists died from the assault rifle's bullets. Daniel stopped running once Mathew took care of the cultists and waited for him to come up.

"Man. You hit the fucking jackpot with that." Daniel said in astoundment.

"Yeah. We should probably get going though. Let me check the bodies for some car keys. With any luck, we'll be able to drive to the cemetery and get there faster." Mathew said as he searched the bodies' pockets.

While Mathew was searching, he suddenly heard a clicking noise behind him and realized Daniel had his gun pointed at him from behind…

"So sorry Matt…but a gun like that should be in the right hands." Daniel said with a smile on his face.

"Daniel…You do realize that I know the handgun is not loaded. You even said so yourself before we even came here that you had no ammo." Mathew said now getting up to face Daniel.

"That's where you are wrong." Daniel said as he shot Mathew in the leg which made Mathew drop down to one knee and the assault rifle fell out of his hands.

"Damnit Daniel!!!! I should have known you weren't completely on my side." Mathew said in pain as he looked at Daniel in anger.

"I'm not on the cult's side neither Matt. I'm on my own side." Daniel said as he kicked Mathew in the face and made him fall to the ground. Daniel then took the assault rifle once he put the handgun in his pants behind him.

"You know something? I really should thank you for getting me this. It will really come in handy once I kill Key and revive the demon king for myself." Daniel said as he pointed the gun at Mathew.

"You don't know what you are talking about! You aren't a demon like Key and-" Mathew said until his face got bashed with the butt of the assault rifle's stock.

"Do you think I care? If he was once human and can do this I can too! I'll prove myself to the demon king I'm more capable than Key to be by his side! Now…enough talk! TIME TO DIE!" Daniel shouted as he pulled the trigger of the assault rifle. However, once Daniel pulled the trigger nothing was happening…

"What the fuck!?" Daniel shouted as he looked over the assault rifle to see what's wrong.

"Looking for this?" Mathew said while holding up the other clip he stashed in his pocket.

Daniel started to put two and two together and realized the clip that was currently in the assault rifle was empty from Mathew shooting it earlier at the other cultists.

"DAMN YOU!!" Daniel shouted as he reached to pull out his handgun but was suddenly ran over by a truck.

Mathew was relieved that he was saved but disheartened when he saw the assault rifle was broken from being ran over by the truck as well.

Suddenly, the truck door opened and emerged another cultist laughing psychotically. Mathew quickly grabbed Daniel's handgun and shot the cultist with the last two bullets within the magazine.

The cultist died but Mathew was again back to square one. However, time was running out because he need to stop Key before it was too late. With no more options Mathew decided to take the truck the cultist had and drive it to the cemetery. Even with no ammo, Mathew took the handgun in case he came across any bullets along the way.

Later on in the night however, Key and Rose finally reached their destination…the cemetery. The dark night had the full moon casting down his light upon a specific mausoleum. Deep in Rose's heart, she knew that Key chose this mausoleum to host the ritual to summon the demon king because this specific mausoleum was where Ghost family was buried.

"This is where the barrier between Earth and Hell is weakest. For generations, the Ghost family has tried to summon the demon king but failed in the attempt. It wasn't until I arrived is when the fool of a mayor tried reasoning with me by offering his only daughter to hopefully be in my good graces and open the doorway." Key explained.

"They were right to go to you my lord." Rose chimed in.

"They were fools dabbling in things they didn't fully understand. However, I know fully well what was needed and thanks to them…we finally have the final piece of the puzzle to open the doorway." Key said as he opened the cemetery gate and a twisted smile came across his face while walking into the cemetery while carrying Eliza and Rose followed.

However, once they reached the mausoleum, a truck came up to the gate and once the door opened Mathew came out. Mathew saw Key and his follower with a girl over his shoulder. He knew time was almost out so he rushed to their location through the graveyard.

"Well well…Look who it is…" Key said as he turned to face Mathew.

"It's over Key! Put the girl down and give yourself up!" Mathew shouted.

"Oh is it? I hate to disappoint you boy but no one can stop me now." Key said as the mausoleum door opened.

"I will stop you! Now stop what you are doing before it's too late!" Mathew demanded.

"Rose my dear…Keep our guest occupied while I prepare the ritual below. Once you deal with him come to me and witness the birth of a new world." Key said and Rose nodded.

After Key carried Eliza into the mausoleum and into its crypt below. Rose was now alone with Mathew as the air around both of them was getting colder. The moon light beamed down upon them and the tension was intense. Rose held her knife she took from the mansion's kitchen from before and Mathew saw the blade which was stained with blood.

"Listen to me! Your leader needs to be stopped! If the demon king is revived then that's it for the world!" Mathew said but Rose just ignored him.

"Please! I'm begging you! You must help me stop Key!" Mathew shouted but was still getting nowhere.

"You know something…after all these years…you still don't know how to look at what's important when it really matters." Rose said as she lifted her hood of her robe and revealed her face to Mathew.

In complete shock Mathew couldn't believe his eyes. His lips were trembling at what he was seeing right now as tears flown down his face…

Without believing in what Mathew saw, the name escaped his mouth… "Sarah."

Chapter 11

Cold air filled the night as the horrifying moment came to pass. Mathew's heart was racing with different emotions but the one he was feeling the most was pain. Pain that the woman he loved was with one person he was trying to stop. However, in a daze Mathew said her name because he still couldn't comprehend what he was seeing...

"Sarah." Mathew said in disbelief as he stood in front of the woman he's been looking for ever since he came to this town.

"Long time no see Mathew. I knew you would come." Rose said.

"How?..." Mathew asked.

"Because I know you and you would do anything just to find me but you know what?...I don't need saving!" Rose shouted.

"Why?..." Mathew asked in a low depressed tone.

"Don't act so surprised. I had planned for you to come here. Your lieutenant at East City Police Department agreed to select you to be sacrificed to the demon king so that all ties with our families and people closest to us would be erased." Rose explained.

"THAT DOESN'T EXPLAIN SHIT!!!!! What the fuck are you doing here!? Why the living hell are you with the cult!? ANSWER ME!" Mathew shouted with in anger after feeling betrayed by the one he loved the most.

"Well for starters, my name isn't Sarah. I've lied to you all these years about my name, my family, and everything you thought you knew about me." Rose said.

"What about your work?! Your studies at college to become a nurse practitioner?!" Mathew demanded.

"I've been with Lord Key the whole time. I lied to you about my life to get your trust. I wanted to bring you myself but I had to get Marcus, your police lieutenant, to send you here." Rose said.

"But isn't this your home town? What about your family?" Mathew asked.

"Hahahahahahaha! My fucking family? Really? Those good for nothing parents tried to stop me but I took care of them." Rose said with an insidious smile on her face.

"…What do you mean?..." Mathew asked but was hesitant about it.

"What do you think dumbass? I killed them for my lord Key!" Rose said.

"…All these years we've been together…meant nothing to you?" Mathew said looking the other way in depression because now he's seen Sarah's true colors.

"Obviously. I told you…You were a means to an end. I hated to spend all that time with you and I loathed pretending to be in love with you. Day after fucking day! All I cared about was Lord Key for showing me a new way in my pathetic life and I would do anything for him!" Rose said gripping her knife tightly.

Tensions between the two were growing. Mathew didn't want to believe right now that this was Sarah he knew before. However, Rose finally felt that this was her chance to take care of a loose end that was a thorn in the cult's side. As the night sky had some clouds that were passing by the moon's light, one cloud finally passed and the light shown once again. In this moment, Mathew decided to speak again in another attempt to end this peacefully…

"Sarah-" Mathew said until the knife Rose had swiped near Mathew's face violently but thankfully Mathew dodged it.

"MY NAME ISN'T FUCKING SARAH!!" Rose screamed as she went after Mathew in an attempt to kill him.

Mathew tried dodging but every now and then Rose's attacks got through. Cuts and nicks reached Mathew's hands, face, and torso. However, Mathew was still hesitant to fight back because he still couldn't make himself believe this was Sarah in front of him that's trying to kill him.

"Please stop!" Mathew begged as he backed up but accidently stepped on awkward rock and fell to the ground face down.

Mathew tried getting back up quickly but before he could, Mathew's leg was stabbed by Rose's knife when she lunged at him to make sure he didn't escape. Pain coursed through his lower left leg but what really hurt Mathew was that Sarah wasn't Sarah anymore. She was now a distant memory and all that remained was a psychotic woman named Rose that was trying to kill him.

"Where do you think you're going!?" Rose shouted as she took out the knife and stabbed Mathew's upper leg when he tried to escape her deathly hold over him.

"GET OFF OF ME!" Mathew shouted as he rolled over and knocked Rose off by kicking her with his good leg.

Rose tried attacking again but Mathew kicked her again in the face to defend himself. Mathew got up and limped fast towards another part of the graveyard. However, once Rose collected herself, she went after Mathew...

"Mathew…Where are you?... I just want to kill you… COME THE FUCK OUT ALL READY!!!" Rose shouted as she kicked a headstone to pieces while searched for Mathew.

Mathew was hiding behind one of the large grave stones in the graveyard. He could hear Rose's voice getting closer and closer but he didn't want to move because he was afraid she might see him.

Suddenly, Mathew spotted the undertaker's house a dozen yards away once the moon light landed on it. He assumed that would be a good place to lose Rose but he really needed to stop Key before it's too late. However, the moon's light was dimming a little and Mathew looked up to see the eclipse had started…

"Shit! I'm running out of time! If Key succeeds in reviving the demon king then the world will be in danger! I have to stop him…at any cost." Mathew thought as the possibility of Rose having to die weighed on his mind.

With no other options at the moment, Mathew decided to rush to the house. However, Rose saw him and chased after Mathew with intention to finish what she started. When Mathew finally reached the house, he busted through the door.

Inside was a shovel near a staircase but before he touched it…

"AHH!!!!!" Mathew screamed in pain because Rose stabbed Mathew in the back.

"How does it feel!? Does it hurt asshole!? I'll make sure there will be more where that came from!" Rose sadistically said as she twisted the knife making Mathew scream even more.

Mathew then elbowed Rose in the gut and grabbed the shovel once freed from her knife. Once Rose tried again to attack Mathew, she was caught off guard from him using the shovel against her face. Rose had fallen to the ground and dropper her knife. She was now looking up at Mathew terrified that he had the upper hand as he looked down on her…

"P-Please! Just let me go. I promise to forget about the cult and Lord Key. I'll never do any harm again! Just let me go…Please Mathew!" Rose begged.

"…Sarah. No…Rose. As much as I want to believe that…this is where we say good bye." Mathew said as he raised the shovel and smacked Rose's face over and over again while she screamed.

Blood splattered with each hit Mathew forced on Rose and tears poured with each heated breath Mathew took. Guilt, shame, sadness, and unimaginable pain overwhelmed Mathew's heart as he fallen to his knees over Rose's body. The very person he was trying to save…The very person he known for years…The very person he loved more than life itself…died from his own hands.

After a few minutes of sitting in remorse, Mathew got up. Dripping with blood, Mathew used the shovel to help him walk. He then picked up Rose's knife because he's going to need it. However, before he walked out of the door…

"Where…do…you…think…you're…going?" Rose said in an altered tone as she got up.

Mathew couldn't believe it, he thought for sure he killed Rose. However, when he turned around, something terrifying stood before him. Rose's eyes were gone and her teeth turned into demonic razors. Her skin, hair, and nails darkened as a deep growl came from her as she breathed. This terrifying transformation frightened Mathew as he was about to run.

Suddenly, this demonic version of Rose charged at Mathew. Mathew swung the shovel but the creature grabbed it while laughing. Mathew was then shoved outside and the demonic creature walked out of the house.

"W-What are you!?" Mathew shouted.

However, the demon before him just ignored his question but snapping the shove and thrown it away. The demon then jumped with impossible strength and pinned Mathew's body to the ground. Black blood from its mouth poured onto Mathew's disturbed face. Luckily, Mathew still had the knife in his hand and used it against the demon's wrist cutting it deeply and made its own blood spray.

"RAAAAAHHHH!!!" The demon shrieked as it grabbed its wrist while in pain.

Mathew used this chance to lung at the demon and stabbed it in the head and twisted the knife for a quick kill. Shaking, Mathew pulled out the knife which was lathered with the demon's dark blood. This was something Mathew couldn't comprehend because he thought demons needed to possess people while they were still alive.

Suddenly, the skies darkened a little more and black clouds swarmed near the half eclipsed moon. Afterwards, dark red lightning blasted from the clouds and wild wind came in all directions. This unnatural storm was nothing the earth had seen before. Mathew was horrified by this sight but what scared him the most was demons bursting out of the ground one by one. Each one either flying away or running out of the cemetery.

At first, Mathew thought they were coming from Hell to kill everything in their sight and create havoc but after seeing them fleeing like they were from the cemetery, Mathew believed they were running from something…

"What could be more terrifying than demons?" Mathew said but then suddenly realized the demon king must be near and Mathew rushed to the mausoleum.

Rose's attacks that she had inflicted on Mathew injured him greatly and he was in so much pain in more ways than one. However, Mathew tried his best to ignore this in order to stop the demon king's revival. Mathew opened the door of the mausoleum then descended down into the dark and vast crypt.

The smell was disgusting and the light was very dim. Mathew could hardly see while going deeper in. However, something warm was nearby and Mathew followed that to what seemed like a hidden room within the mausoleum's crypt.

Once he got to where this large room was, there was a red curtain before it. Behind the curtain, Mathew could hear demonic chanting going on and a bright glow before he opened the curtain. Once he did open the curtain however, something unbelievably terrifying was before him.

"PLEASE!!!! HELP!!" Eliza screamed while she was chained and hanging between two pillars.

Key was in front of her chanting and in front of them both was a massive flame doorway that was what Key was chanting to but soon stopped once he felt Mathew's presence…

"Young Mathew…It seems you have killed my loyal servant." Key said now facing Mathew.

"Key! Stop this at once! Do you know what you are doing?!" Mathew shouted.

"I KNOW EXACTLY WHAT I'M DOING!" Key shouted back but his voice shook the very underground room they were in.

"P-Please!!! Officer Mathew help me!" Eliza begged as unstopping tears flown down her face.

"Don't worry! I'll get you out!" Mathew called out.

"The time is at hand Mathew. The demon king will come to rule all! Three of us are here but only one of us will walk out alive!" Key said as an evil smile crept on his face.

Mathew readied himself for the final fight to stop the revival of the demon king. Every battle Mathew had to endure lead him to this moment. From fighting off the cult, to killing the monsters the cult created, and fight the demons that were now erupting from Hell itself…Mathew knew it all ends right now.

Suddenly, Mathew saw Key's demonic nails burst through Eliza's chest and out her back. Blood splatter and screams echoed inside the tomb as Mathew witnessed Key killing Eliza right in front of him. Key grabbed Eliza's heart from within her body and small dark chains wrapped around the heart making it stay alive. Grabbing the heart tightly, Key turned to face the doorway that lead to Hell.

"Now that I have Lock's heart. I'll walk into the doorway with it. Once I walk back out, I'll become one with Lock and the demon king will be born once again!" Key shouted.

Suddenly, Mathew charged at Key with knife in hand while he was distracted. However, Key saw and moved before Mathew could land a blow. Desperately trying to kill Key, Mathew swung the knife in every direction he could but Key was easily dodging the failed attempts.

"Pathetic!" Key shouted as he back handed Mathew with demonic strength and sent him flying into the wall.

Mathew coughed up blood as he fell to the ground from the cratered wall. However, Key wasn't done as he used his impossible speed to grab Mathew by the neck and lift him into the air. Key's hand choked the very breath out of Mathew while Key gazed into Mathew's eyes with murderous intent.

"I can't believe that you were the wretch that caused so much trouble for me. Rose should have killed you with no problem but I guess she was just too damn WEAK!" Key shouted as he slammed Mathew into the wall again.

"D-D-Damn y-you!" Mathew struggled to say as he hit Key's arm over and over again in attempts to get free but wasn't strong enough to escape Key's grasp.

Suddenly, Key used his magic to levitate the heart he was holding and sent it near the fiery doorway of Hell. He then used his free hand to pierce Mathew's leg and dragged his nails down Mathew's leg. Blood was pouring out and Mathew was in agonizing pain while Key grinned at Mathew's toucher. Burning hellfire scorched Mathew's flesh as he screamed.

"What's wrong little human? Can't take the pain? You'd better get used to it because this sensation is what you are going to feel from now on once I revive the power of the demon king." Key said as he got close to Mathew.

"Sc-Screw you!" Mathew shouted as he head-butt Key and made him back off for a second.

Mathew saw the knife on the ground he had earlier but Key still had his hold on him until he threw

Mathew once again onto the pillars where Eliza's body was hanging. The chains on the pillars broke and Eliza's body was now on the ground along with Mathew. Mathew coughed up blood once again because of his injuries but when he looked up he saw that Key was making his way once again towards the door. Suddenly, the whole tomb was shaking and Mathew saw Key was laughing maniacally.

"It's here! The eclipse is finally here!! The time of reckoning has come to this earth!" Key shouted with enjoyment.

Suddenly, a white mist appeared which startled both Key and Mathew. All of the sudden, ghosts appeared and grabbed ahold of Key. Half of all the ghosts Mathew recognized were people from the town. Tiffany, Susy, James, Harold, and even Eliza were there trying to stop Key. Mathew couldn't believe his eyes but knew they were trying to help him.

It dawned on Mathew that this was his last chance to stop Key so Mathew knew what he had to do. Mathew used all his strength that he had left to get up and rush over to the knife. He then lunged at Key with all his might and stabbed him through the lower jaw up to his head but accidently pushed Key into the portal with himself. However, Key used his nails to pull in the heart with him and Mathew.

Hellfire roared through the portal with Mathew and Key's screams. However, after ten minutes had past the eclipse finally was ending. Suddenly, a figure walked through the door and back into the tomb with a dead body in one hand and a heart in the other. The doorway disappeared once the eclipse was over. The dark figure tossed the body to the ground and walked over to Eliza's body. He placed the heart back within Eliza magically while healing her up and after a few moments she was alive once again.

Breathing heavily, Eliza looked up and saw the man in front of her but terror filled her heart. Horns were all around the dark figure's head like a crown and darkness smoldering out of his back like a cloak. Eliza then recognized the face as tears flown down her face in disbelief and shock…

"Y-You! I-I know you!" Eliza said but the figure walked away and left Eliza down in the tomb alone.

The night was nearly over and the demon king was born but the one whom the power went to wasn't Key…

"All hail the demon king! All hail the demon king!" The rest of the cult chanted as they greeted Mathew out of the tomb with praise.

Suddenly, Mathew lifted his hand and everyone around him burst into bloody explosions. The field was stained with blood and broken bodies laid about everywhere as the flesh has littered the graveyard. The power of the demon king was unbelievably terrifying but took its toll as blood poured down Mathew. Mathew then ascended towards the top of the highest hill in the area and sat down amongst a gravestone…

As the sun finally arisen to its dawn, the light hit Mathew from behind. Since Mathew wasn't a demon, he couldn't keep the form of the demon king when the sun hit him and burned his very soul. However, this wasn't the only pain he was feeling. The nightmares he had faced within the past few days filled his dying heart. He wished none of this had happened and it was all just a bad dream. However, as he gazed his final moments through blood teared eyes…

The last sight he would see was the town of horror…

THE END

Made in the USA
Coppell, TX
08 September 2021